ARES' WAR

Book Two of the Trojan War Cycle

Neil Maresca

ARES, the Greek god of war at the battle of Troy

"Cry 'Havoc!' and let slip the dogs of war."

Julius Caesar
Act 3, Scene 1, line 273

CONTENTS

CRY HAVOC!

MAJOR CHARACTERS

ITHAKANS

Odysseus: King of Ithaka; famous for his wisdom and cunning; a favorite of the Goddess Athena; married to Penelope, and patron of his young cousin, Illotos.

Penelope: Wife of Odysseus

Telemachus: Their infant son.

Illotos: Cousin and ward of Odysseus; steals Demia away from Agamemnon's court and takes her to live with him in Ithaka.

Demia: Youngest daughter of King Kartaxis of Thessolonia; sent by him to the palace at Mycenae; elopes with Illotos.

Lipos: Illotos' companion and protector.

Kretin: Spartan military veteran appointed by Odysseus to turn Lipos and his companions into soldiers.

Eurycleia: Nursemaid to Odysseus when he was a babe and now housemaid to Penelope.

Polybus: Wealthy landowner and moneylender. Enemy of Odysseus. Covets Penelope.

Eurymachus: Son of Polybus. Covets Demia.

GREEKS

Agamemnon: Head of the House of Atreus; King of Mycenae, commander of the largest of the Greek armies, and most powerful of all the Greek kings.

Menelaus: Brother of Agamemnon; King of Sparta, Husband of Helen.

Klytemnestra: Queen of Mycenae; wife of Agamemnon, and sister of Helen.

Helen: The most beautiful woman in all of Greece, a favorite of Aphrodite, the goddess of love; Queen of Sparta (later known as Helen of Troy), wife of Menelaus and sister of Klytemnestra. Abandons her husband and flees to Troy with her lover, Paris.

Achilles: Greatest of the Greek warriors and leader of the Pythians; holds a grudge against the House of Atreus because he believes the brothers, Agamemnon and Menelaus, conspired against him in the competition for Helen's hand in marriage.

Patroclos: Achilles' lover.

Nestor: Elder statesman of Agamemnon's court.

Calchas: Famous oracle of Apollo; rescued from pirates by Odysseus and given by him to King Agamemnon.

TROJANS

Paris: Prince of Troy; favored by Apollo, reputed to be the handsomest man in the world; son of King Priam, brother of Hector and Cassandra; betrothed to Iphigenea. Elopes with Helen, Queen of Sparta.

Hector: Prince of Troy; oldest child of Priam and next in line to inherit the throne. A famous warrior.

Cassandra: Princess of Troy, daughter of Priam and sister of Hector and Paris. Gifted by Apollo with the ability to see the future but deemed a madwoman by all but Hector and Paris.

Aeneas: Trojan military leader; uncle to Paris and Cassandra; known for his dedication to duty, chosen to lead the Trojan delegation to Mycenae for the wedding.

Sinon: A Trojan, recruited by Nestor to spy for Greece.

Cassandra

I hate sailing. I hate the sea. The very thought of a ship makes my stomach turn, but I must admit that when I stepped on board a Trojan ship and turned my back on the barbarian Greeks, I felt nothing but joy. It was bliss. All around me there was activity. Uncle Aeneas strode the deck like a demi-god, barking orders and curses so rapidly that I could not understand the half of them—but the men understood well enough. They moved with speed and purpose, and in no time our ship was away from the dock, the ship's Master wielding his whip with a vengeance, the drum booming a steady rhythm, and the oarsmen beating the waves in perfect unison. As the ship passed out of the rocky harbor, and I saw the deep blue expanse of Poseidon's realm stretching before me uninterrupted all the way to the world's edge, I understood what mariners feel, and why they love the sea so much— *Freedom!* For the first time in my life, I felt free! It was exhilarating! At least until we crested the first swell, and my stomach rebelled against the movement, propelling me to the rail where I quickly discharged the contents of my stomach into the sea. I don't suppose Poseidon appreciated my sacrificial offering, but then who knows the minds of the gods?

I spent the remainder of the trip in bed, never far from my bucket. It was a misery, but I took solace in the fact that I was headed home—although if I had known what awaited me there, I would have not been so content. I grieved for Nefeli, who failed to show up at the boats, and had to be left behind. I wanted to wait for her, or go back and look for her, but Aeneas was unyielding, and so we sailed away without her. I wept to think what fate awaited her. I could only hope that her death was quick and painless. I was certain that the Greeks would show no mercy to any Trojan left behind.

Paris and Helen came to visit me whenever they could spare time from their lovemaking. They spent almost as much time in their bed as I did in mine, although I am sure their time passed much more pleasantly than mine. I enjoyed seeing them—they were so much in love. They carried on like two smitten teenagers. Paris was so happy! He had found what everyone told him was impossible to find—his one, true love. People had mocked him. They would mock him no more. Helen was beautiful. Perhaps because she too was in love; she was radiant. And best of all, she was humble, kind, and open. I think I fell in love with her too. We became close friends. She would confide all sorts of things to me. She told me that, even though she was older than Paris, and had been married for five years, he was the first man she had sex with, and the only man that she had ever loved! I could scarcely believe it, but Helen was honest; there was no deceit in her. She didn't tell me this to brag about her virtue, but to reassure me that her love for Paris was true. She knew there would be hardships, but she believed, naively I thought, that their love would be enough to overcome any obstacles. If only that had proven to be true!

When the ship came to rest in the bay facing Troy, I transferred to a dinghy to come ashore. When I saw the walls of the citadel standing proudly on the strand, I wept and threw myself on the ground. A bit melodramatic, I admit, but it had the intended effect. Hector came, lifted me off the ground, and hugged me tightly. Folded inside his massive arms, I knew I was safe from my father's anger. Paris had told me that Aeneas held me responsible for the entire marriage debacle and had communicated that to the King. I had no doubt that my father would have me tossed back into the sea like an unwanted, inedible fish, but Hector's protective embrace saved me—for a little while at least.

I couldn't cling to Hector forever, and soon after the reception party moved through the massive gates into the citadel, armed guards slipped alongside me and swiftly conveyed me to the dungeon where my father had long threatened to imprison me. It was a filthy disgusting place, every bit as unpleasant as my father promised it would be—a small, dark, dank stone room, sealed with a large oaken door, with no light, crawling with vermin and stinking of urine and feces. I had often defied my father's wishes, and he had just as often threatened me with imprisonment. His threats didn't bother me. I don't know what I imagined. I think I believed I was being heroic, and the threatened imprisonment would be romantic— something like being a princess in a tower in a story. It seems that I was much younger only a few, short days ago. Now, faced with the reality of being shut away underground in a filthy dungeon, I realized that I was a foolish, spoiled child. I also discovered that I am not as brave as I thought I was. I cried. I cried standing up because I was afraid to sit down. I could feel things crawling over my feet and hear their scratching and squealing.

I was standing there crying, petrified, when I heard Hector outside the door. He was shouting curses and threats, and, apparently, beating the guards, because I could hear their pleas for mercy. There was more shouting and whimpering, accompanied by the clatter of keys, and suddenly the big door swung open, and Hector's huge frame filled the doorway, his face a picture of rage.

"Cassandra," he said softly, as his anger melted into grief at the sight of me. "Come. Let us get out of here."

He came forward, lifted my trembling body as if I weighed no more than a feather, and carried me to where I am now, still a prisoner, but far more contented.

My quarters here are not much different than those I occupied in Mycenae. There it was considered luxury. Here it is reserved for prisoners of the upper classes who are awaiting trial or execution. The apartment—for it consists of four rooms—is in a remote corner of the palace, a corner never visited by the King or any member of the royal court. Hector told me that I would be safe here as long as I did not show my face outside the doors. So I am still confined, but in truth I do not really mind. I can receive visitors, should any care to risk the wrath of the King. None but Hector, Paris, and Helen dare, but that is all right. I have no need of any others. My own true love, Antenor, is far away, perhaps even dead, and even if he is still alive, he is dead to me. I am certain that I will never see him again.

And whether I am here in this apartment, or in a dungeon, the end will be the same. Apollo has cursed me with a vision of what is to come, and nothing now can change it. I am tortured by the thought of something my uncle said when I told him about my vision. He asked if the vision were a certainty or just a possibility. I dismissed his idea at the time, but I have since wondered whether he is wiser than I thought. The young are sometimes too quick to reject the ideas of their elders as old-fashioned or merely silly. Was I too proud to heed the advice of a man whose judgement all agree is sound? After all, I do not pretend to understand the workings of the gods. I have no doubt that Apollo can see into the mind of Zeus, who knows all things. And I also have no doubt that the vision he sent me is an accurate portrayal of the future—but whose future? Perhaps Zeus, in his wisdom, can see all possible futures, and Apollo sent me one possibility, a possibility that I made a certainty though my actions. If that is the case, then I am responsible not only for my own captivity, but for the death of poor, sweet, Nefeli, and the destruction of Troy.

Miserable creature that I am, I am too weak and cowardly to take my own life, so I sit here in solitude, weeping for those I love whose lives I may have destroyed.

* * *

Paris stopped by a week or so ago, all excited about the arrival of a peace delegation from Greece.

"Can the peace be saved?" I asked after he had seated himself and sipped the wine that the servant brought us.

"I doubt it," he said. "The Greeks are demanding the return of Helen, who they claim was abducted, and they want monetary compensation as well as trade concessions.

"Ah, money," I said. "What price are they putting on Helen's virtue?"

"An absurd amount, but that is merely a starting point for negotiations."

"Who is leading the Greek delegation?"

"Nestor."

"He seems to be a good man."

"He is, but the Greeks have also sent Patroclos along with him, and Helen tells me that he is not a good man."

"Helen is right. He is Achilles' lover, and Achilles wants war. His presence is not a good sign."

"It doesn't matter. I'm not giving up Helen, and she has no wish to return to Greece."

"But will father support you? War is not a pretty thing."

"No, it is not, and I wish there were some other way. I suppose if the Greeks would drop the demand that she return, it could be worked out, but as long as they insist on 'rescuing' Helen, I don't see what can be done."

"It can be done, if father insists that it be done. I imagine that all of the merchants are pushing for some sort of accommodation."

"Oh, yes. They are very unhappy, and they have made life miserable for Helen and me."

"How so?"

"We are insulted by the common people in the streets and snubbed by our own class at every social occasion."

"Can nothing be done about this?"

"Hector has assigned guards for our protection from the mob, but they can do nothing about the social insults and affronts. I believe only Hector stands between us and the Greeks. The people have no taste for war, especially one fought over what they refer to as a Greek whore."

"That is terrible. What does father say?"

"What he always says—nothing. He is far too busy with his concubines to take any interest in matters of state."

"How many does he have now?"

"I don't know. Over 80 I think."

"What can he possibly do with them? He is far past any sexual acts. I'm not sure he could even remember what to do, much less summon up the strength to do it."

"It would be funny if it weren't so tragic. Thank the gods that we have Hector."

"Yes. I am sure he saved my life. Do you think he can save Troy as well?"

"I don't know, but if the Greeks are reasonable, Hector will find a way. I fear this Patroclos fellow. I barely recall meeting him, but I remember that he struck me as false. Helen tells me that he is sly, and much too taken with himself."

"Yes. That fits my memory of him. His vanity is his weakness. Tell Hector. That might help."

"I will, but now I must go. I have neglected Helen for too long."

"Brother, it has been barely an hour. Surely she can bear to be apart from you for that long?"

"You have found me out, sister. It is not she, but me who cannot bear to be apart."

"Then fly to her and bring my love along with you."

* * *

Things have gone from bad to worse. The two parties have agreed on an apology from Paris, along with significant financial and commercial incentives. The sticking point is Helen. The Greeks, specifically Patroclos and the group he represents, insist on Helen's return. Ironically, Nestor, who speaks for Agamemnon and Helen's husband Menelaus, does not.

Helen will not return to Greece. She says she will kill herself before she abandons Paris. What is there for her in Greece? Shame? Humiliation? Probably worse. I have been told that the penalty for adultery in Sparta is stoning. Can you imagine—*stoning?* The Greeks are truly despicable.

There is a great deal of pressure on Priam to give in to the Greeks' demands. Nobody, aside from Paris, Hector, and me, cares for Helen. Even Andromeda, Hector's wife, will have nothing to do with her. Helen is probably the most hated person in the entire Trojan empire. Only Hector stands between her and exile to Greece.

The problem of course, is money. Nobody really cares about Helen. If the merchants and bankers had not already invested heavily in the economic returns of a merger between Greece and Troy, then Paris could have married Medusa, and nobody would have blinked. He could have brought her and her Gorgon head to the King's ball, and they all would have greeted her with smiles. But fortunes were wagered on the success of the marriage between Paris and Iphigenea, and those fortunes are now in great jeopardy.

Hector knows this, and that is why he protects Helen. He sees it for what it is, and he refuses to let the speculators dictate policy. He told me the other day that he had made a fair offer, one that was acceptable to King Agamemnon, and that Patroclos' insistence on Helen's return was unnecessary and unacceptable.

"It is meant to humiliate us. Nothing more," he said. "It serves no practical purpose. Her husband does not insist upon it. In fact," he said, "Nestor told me that he wishes her well, and hopes that she is happy with Paris, as she never was with him."

"So why doesn't Agamemnon silence Patroclos? I can't believe he wants war."

"Agamemnon and his brother are alone. Achilles, Diomedes, Ajax and all the other Greek leaders are demanding war as a matter of honor. He cannot appear to be weak."

"Where is Odysseus? Won't he help?'

"Odysseus is on Ithaka with his wife and new–born babe. Nestor says he wants to live in peace and has refused all pleas to return to Mycenae and the Council."

"Then all is lost. There will be war."

"I am afraid so. Our spies report that even as they negotiate, they are building their armies and preparing for war."

"And what are we doing?"

"I have placed Aenaes in charge of organizing the armies and preparing the defenses."

"Defenses? You think they will attack Troy?"

"They will have to. We will not engage them at sea where they are superior. They will have to sail here and face us on land. Our people have little taste for this war, but if they see an invading force on our land, they will rally."

"You will let them bring their forces here unimpeded?"

"Yes. Once they are here, they will have no place to go. They cannot breach these walls. They are miles and miles away from supplies and reinforcements. Our naval forces can blockade the bay to prevent relief. They will soon see the futility of their adventure. They will have to go home or starve to death on the beach."

"I hope you are right. I have seen terrible visions..."

"Your visions are not always to be trusted. Place your trust instead in me and these walls. As long as both stand, you and Troy are safe."

* * *

I had a vision last night—the most terrifying that I have ever had. There was no blood, no battles, no horrible scenes of death and destruction, just a horse—a wooden horse, finely wrought. It did nothing. It just stood there, but it filled me with dread. For some reason, I knew the Greeks had built it. In my dream it moved—not exactly *moved*; that is, its legs didn't move. The whole structure moved, as if it were on a wheeled cart. At first there was no sound, but then I heard rejoicing, a crowd appeared. They surrounded the horse, singing and dancing. But I was afraid. The gates of the citadel swung open. The horse's face grew larger and larger, and I saw that it was grinning. It opened its mouth and laughed. I screamed and fell to the floor foaming at the mouth like a wild animal. My maids heard my scream and ran into the room. One look at me writhing on the floor, frothing at the mouth, soiling my garments, and muttering like a madwoman, and they turned around and ran out, adding their screams to my wild sounds.

When I awoke, I was in my bed. I had been washed, and dressed in clean clothes. Two women I did not know were rubbing my arms with cool, wet clothes, and Hector was seated at the side of the bed.

"You have returned to us," he said. "For a time, I feared that you had left us forever."

"I had a vision..."

"You had a 'Falling Down.' It gave you a nightmare. That is all."

"No, there was no dream. I was awake when the vision came. It terrified me so much that the 'Falling Down' followed."

Hector looked at me like a parent looks at a child who has an overactive imagination. I could tell that he wanted to say something, but he refrained. He smiled at me, kissed me on the cheek, and told me to rest. He said he could not stay, there was much to do. He didn't say what, but he didn't have to. I understood.

"Can Paris and Helen come to visit?" I asked.
He seemed reluctant to answer, but finally, he said, "I am afraid not. They are barricaded in their home. It is not safe for them to travel the streets."

"Go then," I said. "Do what you must. May the gods protect you."

"And you as well," he said, and left me in the care of the two nurses.

After he left, the women continued to fuss over me. They are older than the maids who ran away, and kinder, but I wished to be alone, so I dismissed them.

I did not tell Hector about the horse. I know he would not have believed me anyway. I am ashamed. I cannot hold back the tears. I miss Nefeli.

* * * *

Illotos

I am the happiest man alive. I do not say that aloud because I fear the gods, who are a jealous lot, but I whisper it into the ear of my sweet Demia as we make love in the stillness of the night under a star-filled sky. And I whisper it to her again in the morning as we make love to a chorus of birds' singing praises to the rising sun.

She has proven to be a treasure beyond my dreams. I feared she would not be content with a simple life, one without the luxuries she enjoyed in her father's palace. I feared that her love for me would fade in the face of the reality of life with a shepherd-farmer on a barren island far from civilization.

Lipos, Snake, and the others all told me I was making a mistake—that I shouldn't gamble my happiness on a spoiled brat who was far above my class and would soon tire of me. They said I was too young to tie myself down to one woman, no matter how pretty. "The world is full of wenches," they said, and maybe it is, but I have no desire for wenches. I have Demia. I will leave the wenches to others.

The last six months have been hard work. I returned to my home to find most of it in sad condition. The shepherds had gone off, leaving my small stock to the wolves. The few sheep that survived were sickly. When my mother fell ill and was not able to manage the farm, the farmhands also walked off. This was the work of my enemies, Polybus, and his son, Eurymachus. It was the same strategy they used to bankrupt my father. After two years of drought, my father turned to Polybus for a loan. Once he had my father in his debt, he drove off the shepherds and farmhands through bribes and threats, causing my father to default on the loan. He then claimed the land in payment of the debt. All that was left to us was the land that had been my mother's dowry, and still remained in her name.

But my mother's land contained the best pasture, and Polybus was furious when he realized that it was not to be included in the payment of my father's debt. In his anger, he threatened to throw us off the land and take it by force, but he had not reckoned on Odysseus, who is my mother's nephew. As long as Polybus had a legal basis to claim my father's land, Odysseus could not act, but when he threatened to use force against my mother, Odysseus gathered his forces and forced Polybus to back down. That was many years ago, when I was but a child, but Polybus has never forgotten his disgrace, and has continued to plot against Odysseus and me ever since.

So, as soon as Odysseus and I left for Mycenae, he moved against my mother, using his favorite weapons, bribes and threats, to drive off her workers and force the farm into failure. The plan might have worked, except that two of mother's long-time servants, Phenius and Caron, remained loyal, and held the farm together until Odysseus and I returned from Mycenae.

When I heard what had happened, I put on my armor, gathered Lipos and a few others, and headed into town to settle things once and for all. I was about half-way there when I came across Odysseus and Kretin standing in the road.

"Where are you going, Illotos?" Odysseus asked.

"You well know where I am going cousin. Have you come to join us?"

"I wish that I could, but you well know that I cannot. I am King of this rocky isle only because people believe that they can count on me to enforce the peace fairly—which, in this case, means stopping my young cousin from committing murder."

"Polybus' death is not murder. It is justice."

"Leave justice to the gods. It us not for you to decide who lives or dies."

"I wonder whether you would be so forgiving if it were your home and lands that had been threatened, as mine have been."

"People make threats all the time, Illotos. Threats can be ignored. Actions are different. If Polybus had tried to take possession of your lands unlawfully, you can be certain that I and all the forces at my command would stand by your side."

"I would rather not wait for Polybus to decide the time to strike. You always told me that I should not let my enemies dictate the terms of battle."

"And we will not. Here is what I want you to do. Take Kretin and Lipos. Dismiss the others. Confront Polybus. Tell him that any further attempt upon your property will cost him his life. Say no more. Do not let him provoke you to violence."

"Do you think words will stop him?"

"No, but he will see Kretin, and he will know that I stand behind your words. That will stop him."

I knew he was right. I really had no intention of killing Polybus. As much as I would have liked to, I knew it was wrong—and foolish. So when Odysseus offered me an alternative, I gladly accepted it, although I pretended to be unhappy.

Odysseus gathered up my men while Kretin, Lipos, and I marched into town and straight up to Polybus' front door. I drew my sword and banged repeatedly on the door until it was opened by a skinny, frightened servant backed by two armed men.

"Tell your master," I said to the frightened man, "that Illotos, son of Cretias, wishes to speak with him."

"And what if he does not want to speak with you?" huffed one of the armed men.

At that point, Lipos burst through the door, through the servant and into the braggart. Kretin followed immediately behind, and in the time it takes a cobra to strike, they had both men on the ground, disarmed and begging for their lives.

The servant proved to be amazingly quick for a scrawny broomstick of a man. He was off the floor and out of sight before I could stop him. It is amazing how fast a man can run when he is in fear for his life.

A few seconds later, Polybus burst into the room, accompanied by his son, Eurymachus, and two more armed servants.

"Is this the way you greet all your guests?" I asked, as pleasantly as I could manage.

"What do you want? Why are you here?" a red-faced Polybus blustered.

"I am here to speak with you," I answered, "and I want to tell you that any further threats against my mother or me will result in bloodshed—yours."

"Are you threatening me?" he blustered, angrily.

"No. Threats are your domain. That was a promise."

"Oh. I see that little Illotos has grown into a big man— in the shadow of his great cousin," Eurymachus snickered.

"I see no cousin here," I answered.

"But this is his Spartan slave, is it not?" Eurymachus said, indicating Kretin.

It is never a good idea to call any Spartan, 'slave,' but it is a very bad idea to call Kretin anything but 'Sir.' I have practiced with Kretin, and I know how fast his sword is. I thought I was going to see Eurymachus slivered before my eyes, but Kretin did not move. He merely fixed Eurymachus with a hard stare that made him tremble and turn ashen. Eurymachus looked like a man who had seen his own death. I thought of many things I could have said to him, but decided that further words were unnecessary. The message had been delivered.

Polybus tried to save his son further embarrassment. "Get out!" he shouted. "Get out of my house before I have you thrown out!"

The two men who stood alongside of Polybus exchanged nervous glances and looked none too anxious to engage with Lipos and Kretin.

"As you wish, Polybus," I said. "I will leave your house. Make sure you give me no reason to return."

When we were outside, Kretin said to me, "When the time comes, Eurymachus is mine."

* * *

I returned home to hugs, tears, and kisses, as both Demia and my mother took turns clasping me to them and making me promise never to do anything so foolish again.

I promised, although I knew that in my newly acquired role as head of the family that there would likely be other times that such 'foolishness' would be necessary. I was not convinced that Polybus' avarice had been permanently curtailed. He is like a man enamored with wine. He can stay away for a time, but he always returns to his one true love.

But I had no time to worry about Polybus. There was far too much work to be done on the farm to be worried about a low life like him. There were fields to be cleared and planted, pastures to be reclaimed, fences to build, and a hundred and one repairs to be made to the house, which had been sadly neglected since my father's death. I couldn't have done it without the help of Lipos and the other lads. Even Kretin showed up one day to help—although he barked more orders than he did work. Odysseus sent some of his hands to help in the fields, and he gave us two prize rams to help replenish my flock. He even sent over a cook, a housekeeper, and a maid to help my old mother and young bride manage the household. But the greatest help was Demia. She is a wonder!

I don't know what she sees. When we first arrived, I was dismayed, embarrassed, and afraid. Ithaka is a rocky, barren island. Life here is hard, and I feared it would be too hard for someone like Demia, who was raised in a royal palace, and was used to a life of ease. But she stepped off the ship and declared it 'beautiful.' I have never thought of Ithaka as beautiful. It is my homeland, and I love it. I would fight to defend it, but 'beautiful'? Not really.

But to Demia it was beautiful. In fact, everything to Demia was beautiful. She cried when I took her to my home. I thought it was because it was so dilapidated and neglected. But this too, she declared 'beautiful.' She embraced my mother, who declared her to be 'beautiful.' They both wept, and declared that I, too, was 'beautiful.' I thought they had both gone mad.

But Demia was right. I see it now. The beauty is not in the land or the structures that sit on it, but in the love that we share. It is us—me, Demia, and mother—who make this place beautiful. Mostly it is Demia. She transforms everything she touches. Only a short time ago, I had dreamt of glory, of going off like Heracles, to do great deeds, or to excel in battle like the heroes of old, but now I only wish to pass my life here, with Demia and however many children we may be blessed with. Odysseus, too, seems content with his life. He and Penelope are devoted to little Telemachus, who they spoil terribly.

For six months we lived in paradise. Then it all changed. We had received regular messages from Odysseus' agents in Mycenae, so we knew what was going on. We knew that the peace mission had failed. Agamemnon had begged Odysseus to return to the council in Mycenae, but he refused, being unwilling to leave his wife and son. We also knew that Agamemnon had been forced, much against his will, to call for war against Troy. But these events seemed far away, and in our bliss we thought they did not concern us.

We had gathered at Odysseus' villa to celebrate Telemachus' first half-year of life. Everyone was there, including Odysseus' father, Laertes, and Eurycleia, Odysseus' aged nurse, who continuously fussed over the baby. Eumaeus, the head shepherd and Philoetius, the property manager were also there along with Kretin, Lipos, and Charis, who had helped Demia escape Mycenae. It was a special day, even more so for me and Demia, who had our own special reason for celebration.

Lipos stood aside and seemed ill at ease. It was odd, even amusing, to see him shyly accepting a drink from the young maid, Melantho, completely lost, sweating profusely, and no doubt wishing he were in the tavern with his mates, anywhere, in fact, other than where he was.

Melantho had been employed by Penelope while Odysseus was in Mycenae. Demia and Charis immediately disliked her.

"She is untrustworthy," Demia said.

"She is wanton," Charis said.

I was tempted to come to the girl's defense—after all, they had just met her. But I thought better of it, and I'm glad I did, for they turned out to be right. Although, for the life of me, I do not know how they could correctly judge her character after only one glance.

However, all thoughts of Lipos and Melantho evaporated when Odysseus and Penelope entered the atrium holding Telemachus aloft, his head crowned with a laurel leaf. Wine was poured; we spilled a drop onto the ground in respect of our ancestors and toasted the little hero. Then he was passed from hand to hand, admired, fondled, and kissed, never far from the protective presence of Eurycleia, who watched over him like a guardian spirit.

Demia was pregnant. She had suspected it for a time, but we waited until she was certain before making it public. We thought that this celebration would present a good opportunity to break the news to everybody at one time. We were bubbling over with excitement but held our tongues until we could find a suitable time to share our news. After a time, Eurycleia took Telemachus off for a nap, the party quieted down, and we thought that we could reveal our news without intruding upon Odysseus' and Penelope's celebration.

However, our grand moment never came. It was preempted by the arrival of a messenger from Mycenae. The man showed up exhausted from his run from the port—a long and primarily uphill trek. He stumbled into the middle of the party and fell to the ground. Odysseus picked him up and brought him into the shade, while the maid Melantho gave him some water. When the man had recovered enough to speak, he delivered the most amazing message.

"The King is coming," he said.

"Which king?" Odysseus asked. "Coming where? Here?"

At first I thought he meant Demia's father, King Kartaxis. I couldn't think any other king that would have any reason to visit Ithaka. But I was wrong.

"The Great King, Agamemnon," the man said to our amazement.

"Agamemnon is coming?" Odysseus muttered in disbelief. "Here?"

"Yes," the messenger answered.

"When?"

"He is but a day or two behind me."

"WHAT?"

"He sent me ahead to give you ample time to prepare for his arrival."

"AMPLE TIME! AMPLE TIME! ARE YOU MAD? A DAY OR TWO TO PREPARE FOR THE KING?"

I don't think I had ever seen Odysseus so angry. He took the messenger by the neck and lifted him off the ground so high that his feet kicked in the air.

"WHAT DID HE TELL YOU?" Odysseus screamed into the man's reddening face. "WHY IS HE COMING HERE?" WHY WAS I NOT TOLD OF THIS BEFOREHAND?"

If the poor man knew the answers to any of Odysseus' questions, he could not utter them with Odysseus' strong hands wrapped tightly around his throat. He gurgled. He kicked. He furiously waved his hands, but he said nothing. Disgusted, Odysseus threw him to the ground, and stormed away. Just as well, I thought. In a few more minutes the man would have been dead.

Penelope asked Melantho to look after the man, and then hurried to catch up to Odysseus.

"What does this mean?" Demia asked, tears already beginning to form in the corners of her eyes.

"I do not know, my sweet. But it does not bode well."

"What would you have me do, husband?" she asked. I noticed that both of her hands were wrapped protectively across her belly.

"Go home. Melantho is taking care of the King's messenger. Penelope and Odysseus do not need our presence at this time, and I see the men gathering together. I had best join them. Go home. I will tell you all that transpires as soon as I am able to join you."

Demia pulled me close. "I am frightened, Illotos."

"There is no need," I said. "Odysseus will sort it all out. Don't worry." But I didn't believe a word that I had said.

* * *

Two days later, I stood at attention with the rest of the honor guard as Agamemnon's ship docked, and the Great King made his way down the gangplank into the waiting arms of Odysseus' father, Laertes. Nobody had seen Odysseus since he stormed away into his home two days earlier. There were strange rumors circulating that he had gone mad. I did not believe them, but many people did. It was true that he had barricaded himself in his house and none were allowed in except for Penelope and Laertes, but I knew Odysseus too well to believe the rumors. I was sure that he had some trick up his sleeve, although what it was, or *why* it was necessary, I did not know.

Laertes and Agamemnon greeted each other with the traditional hugs and kisses, but I wondered just how sincere each man was. Agamemnon is a politician and not to be trusted, while Laertes is the father of the most cunning man in Greece. Odysseus must have learned his tricks from someone, and if not Laertes, then who?

Laertes escorted Agamemnon to the 'Royal Carriage,' a hastily re-constructed donkey cart that everybody pretended was not a donkey cart. He and Agamemnon climbed up and Snake, the Royal Coachman, whipped the donkeys into a fast trot, bouncing the cart around so violently that most of the decorations had fallen off long before it reached Odysseus' villa.

I had the pleasure of riding with Nestor, a man for whom I had, at the time, a great deal of respect. I picked him out among the crowd of retainers that followed Agamemnon. When I saw that he was having trouble with the swaying, uneven gangplank, I went to his aid.

"Allow me to help you," I said.

He looked up at the sound of my voice and said, "Illotos! It is so good to see you again. I hoped that we would meet."

"You remember me?"

"Of course. Who could forget the dashing young man who stole the second most beautiful woman in all of Greece right out from under the nose of the Great King himself. You may not know it, but you are something of a hero in Mycenae. There is even a song about you and Demia."

"What do you mean, 'the second most beautiful woman'?"

Nestor laughed. "Of course. You are right to insist that Demia is the most beautiful woman on Earth. How is she? Are you two happy?"

"She is with child, and we are both immensely happy. But do not mention the child. We have not told anyone yet."

"My congratulations to you both, and do not worry. I am a diplomat. I know how to keep a secret."

We had reached an empty cart—Odysseus, or Laertes, had arranged for an entire fleet of them to transport Agamemnon's crew of servants and sycophants, who were all grousing and complaining about being in the 'sticks,' and having to ride in donkey carts, which were still—they snidely pointed out—donkey carts, no matter how gaily they had been decorated.

Nestor looked at the cart and laughed. "I see Odysseus is up to his old tricks," he said, but he made no effort to climb into the cart, for it was impossible for him to lift his old limbs high enough, so I picked him up and placed him in his seat.

"You have changed, Illotos," he said once he was comfortable.

"Changed? How so?"

"You are a man now, with broad shoulders and strong arms, and a degree of self-confidence that was not evident in Mycenae."

I don't know about the self-confidence, but it was true that six months of hard work in the fields had added muscle to my body. I had always been athletic, but I was lean then. Now, my frame had filled out and was solid. Demia noticed it too and liked to tease me. "I see," she said, "that your time in bed with me has been well spent. Your body is now hard all over, not just in one small part as it had been when we first met."

The little vixen was incorrigible.

It's amazing how my thoughts always wandered from the matter at hand to Demia. I was still daydreaming about her when Nestor asked, "What game is Odysseus playing today?" He asked quite pleasantly, as if it were idle chatter. I suspected nothing.

"I have no idea," I answered.

"So you do not think he is mad?"

"I do not know, but I doubt it. It is not like Odysseus to give in to his emotions. But if you had seen him the day the King's emissary arrived, you might well believe him mad."

"But you do not think so?"

"No."

"Why not?"

"Because the road is never straight with Odysseus."

"I believe you may be right."

We sat in silence for a while longer before he again asked a question.

"He has a child, does he not? I seem to recall that he was very worried about Penelope when he was in Mycenae. She was in her last month, if I remember correctly."

"Yes. He has a son, Telemachus. Odysseus dotes on the boy."

"Really," he said and grew quiet again.

We rode in silence for a while before Nestor fell asleep and snored the rest of the way.

* * *

Upon arrival outside the walls of Odysseus' villa, we abandoned our donkey carts, and walked through the gates into the courtyard, where the women greeted Agamemnon and his retinue with platters of fruit and pitchers of wine. The refreshments were welcome after the long, hot, uphill ride in the dusty, uncomfortable mule carts, and it was a little while before Agamemnon and the others realized that Odysseus was not there to greet them.

"What is the meaning of this?" Agamemnon demanded of Laertes. "Where is Odysseus? Why is he not here?"

"My Lord," Laertes answered in muted terms. "There is a reason for his absence, which you will learn in a short time, if you will be patient."

Patience was not Agamemnon's strong suit, especially when he sensed an affront to his dignity. In his mind, Odysseus' absence was an inexcusable outrage, and he was about to land all the authority he possessed on the head of poor old Laertes when Nestor intervened. He pulled Agamemnon aside, and whispered something in his ear that seemed to mollify him.

Thank the gods for Nestor, I thought at the time, but later came to regret my words.

"If Odysseus is unable to come to greet me," Agamemnon said, much more kindly, "perhaps you can take us to him?"

"Certainly," Laertes replied, and as he turned toward the villa, he glanced back at me, motioning that I should come as well.

Agamemnon, Nestor, Laertes, and I entered Odysseus' home and stared into the darkness. There was no fire in the hearth. Nor was there any fire in the braziers. We wandered from the entry to the main hall, which was also in darkness. In the darkest corner of the dark room there was a man, sitting in the chair that I knew was Odysseus' favorite. We approached him with some trepidation, not knowing what to expect. Agamemnon paused, and looked at Laertes, but Laertes said nothing, so he moved closer, and we all followed.

The man seated in the corner was Odysseus, but it was not Odysseus. That is; it was not Odysseus as any of us had ever seen him before. The man before us looked like a wild beast. His hair and beard were uncombed and stood out at odd angles from his head and face. He was wearing only a torn and dirty dressing gown, His hands and face, likewise, were scratched, bloody and covered with grime. His head rolled from side to side, and his hands trembled. He looked up at us but seemed not to see us; his eyes rolled in his head, and he muttered words we could not understand.

"What is he saying?" Agamemnon asked.

"We do not know," answered Laertes. "The language is unknown to us."

"How long has he been thus?"

"In this state, only two days, but in truth, he had been acting strange since he returned from Mycenae six months ago."

"It is sad to see such a great man brought so low."

I was stunned. I could not believe what was before my eyes.

Nestor, who seemed unmoved by Odysseus' condition, said, "Wait."

I was about to ask, *Wait for what,* but before I could speak I was interrupted by an ungodly scream, and the clatter and crash as one of the King's soldiers burst into the room holding Telemachus aloft with one hand and brandishing a sword in his other. My hand went to my sword, but once again I was too slow. Odysseus was up and out of his chair faster than my eye could see. He snatched the child from the soldier with his left hand, and with his right drove his fist so hard into the man's chest that his bronze armor buckled, his chest bone cracked, and he dropped to the floor dead. Penelope, all tears, burst through the door into Odysseus' arms. My hand was still on my sword, and had Laertes not stilled it, I would have killed a King and a counselor that day.

Nestor was the first to speak. "It is over Odysseus," he said. "It is time to put away the games and get down to business."

I burned with shame, for it was I who told Nestor that Odysseus was not mad, and I who told him how much he loved his son; and the crafty old man had used these things against Odysseus.

I was twice a fool. Once for not trusting Odysseus, and twice for trusting Nestor. I should have realized that Odysseus was feigning madness with good reason, even if I did not know why. And I also should have realized that a crafty man like Nestor does not engage in idle conversation. It has been a hard lesson, but one I have learned well.

After Agamemnon and his court left, I confessed my shame, and threw myself on Odysseus' mercy. He drew me to him and comforted me.

"You have done nothing wrong," he said. "You did not tell Nestor anything that he did not already know. He has spies everywhere, and I have no doubt that he has them here as well. He was merely confirming what others had already told him."

I recalled that Odysseus had once told me that Nestor was not only Greece's best diplomat, but also its best spy. Odysseus' words helped, but I continued to judge myself more harshly than he did.

* * *

That night, Demia and I took comfort, not pleasure, in each other's arms. She laid her head on my chest and wept, but her tears were not the only ones to stain the sheets. I cried too, for our paradise was coming to an end.

Agamemnon had not undertaken the long, hard journey from his comfortable palace in Mycenae to the sparse, rocky island of Ithaka for his pleasure. Odysseus understood that immediately. As soon as the messenger arrived outside his door, Odysseus knew what was happening. It was one thing for him to claim hardship, and refuse to attend the council, but it was another to refuse to honor his oath to fight alongside the Great King and the other kings and princes of Greece who were gathering to attack Troy.

Torn between his love for his family and his duty to the King, Odysseus had chosen his family. But, because he could not do this openly, he feigned madness—a ruse that might have worked had it not been for Nestor's web of spies, who had kept him apprised of everything that was happening on Ithaka.

One of those spies turned out to be Melantho, who had to be dismissed for disgracing herself with one (or more) of Agamemnon's guards, and, on her way out the door, bragged openly about her treachery. So, it turned out that Demia and Charis were both right—Melantho was both wanton and untrustworthy.

"Why did he not tell you of his plan?" Demia asked when I confessed my foolishness to her. "Doesn't he trust you? It would have spared you some embarrassment and needless guilt."

"He said that he didn't want to involve me in a plan that could be deemed treasonous. He also said that if he were to be charged with treason, he wanted to make sure that I would be left to care for Telemachus and Penelope."

Demia seemed unconvinced. "Still," she said, "it would have been better if you had known the plan."

"Perhaps," I answered, "but it matters not now. The die has been cast. Odysseus must provide ten ships to the united Greek fleet."

"So many!"

"Yes. It may bankrupt him, but he has no choice. Nor do I. Odysseus owes allegiance to Agamemnon, and I owe allegiance to him."

"But that does not mean that you must go to war!" she said, raising her head from my chest and looking into my eyes. "If you ask Odysseus to stay at home, you know he will say yes."

"I cannot do that."

"No! You would rather go off and play the hero than stay here and protect your wife and child!"

"That is unfair, Demia. I would be mocked for a coward..."

"Not by me. Not by those who know you. Is that it? Is it your pride that makes you abandon us?"

"Perhaps. Perhaps it is pride, but I think of it as both more and less than that. It is my reputation, my good name—the name my father gave to me, and the name I must pass on to our child. Would you want that name sullied? Would you want our child to grow up scorned and ridiculed for his father's cowardice? You may not think ill of me now, but what of the future when you see our family outcast? Would you not think it better if I had gone to war and never returned?"

Demia placed her head back on my chest.

"It is a hard choice," I said. "There is no easy path."

"I know," she whispered, and buried her head further into my chest.

* * *

I said farewell to Demia this morning. She cried piteously and clung to me so hard that I had to tear her hands away from my garments. It was the hardest, cruelest thing I have ever done. Had Lipos not come, placed his hand on my shoulder, and led me away, I don't think I could have left her.

Odysseus was waiting for us on board his trireme, newly outfitted, and looking trim and bold. He had all his ships painted black, and the prows draped with long, black hair out of which came two long, white fangs. From the front, the ships resembled huge wild boars, the strongest, most ferocious, and unpredictable of beasts, and would no doubt instill terror in any Trojan sailor watching the huge, three-tiered ship bearing down on him at high speed.

Odysseus sacrificed to the Master of the Sea, Poseidon, and to his protectress, Athena, and then we set off with everybody at the rail looking back as we left the harbor, all wondering if we would ever live to see Ithaka and our loved ones again.

* * * *

Patroclos

Achilles is in high spirits. He paces back and forth like a finely trained thoroughbred waiting for the race to begin. He is going to war, and he has dragged the entire Greek nation along with him. He couldn't be happier. Most of the remainder of the Greek nation (if there is such a thing) is not so excited. Nobody really cares about Helen, not even her husband, but Achilles went on so long about 'the honor of Greece' and the 'insult to the nation' that nobody dared oppose him for fear of being called a coward. He has his supporters, of course. Diomedes and Ajax went around waving their fists in the faces of all who opposed war. I would say they were half-wits, but that is giving them too much credit. But they are fearsome, and nobody, not even the 'Great King' himself wants to anger them. The only man who could have faced them down is Odysseus, and he stayed home. Here is one of the world's great ironies: Odysseus wants peace, and he might have had it if he had left his wife and child and come to the council hall in Mycenae. Now I understand he is on his way here to join the 'United Greek army." What a joke that is. They can't even agree on what to have for breakfast. It took more than eight months to assemble this 'army,' and now that it is almost here, nobody can agree on what to do with it.

The bickering started the day after Helen left, and it has continued unabated from then until now. Paris' abduction of Helen (if she was abducted) threw everyone into a frenzy. There is no word to describe what happened here except 'insanity.' First everybody blamed everybody else for the breakdown in security. Achilles wanted to drag out all of the guards and torture them until they revealed who had bribed them with women and wine until I reminded him that I had been responsible, and I had acted on his orders. Agamemnon had several of the guards executed, but the Captain was spared, and since he was the only one who knew the truth, so was I.

Then they started fighting over Achilles' slaughter of the Trojans who had been left behind, most of whom were innocent servants and slaves. Achilles had gone mad when he learned of Helen's kidnapping. He vowed to kill every Trojan on earth, and he started with those immediately at hand. I once tried suggesting that Helen might have left of her own free will, but the very idea of it threw him into a violent rage. His pride would not allow him to believe that Helen would prefer a 'little boy' to him. Losing her to Menelaus in a rigged contest was one thing. Having her choose someone over him was another.

Actually, I found the idea very plausible. Paris is a very pretty 'little boy.' I could have been tempted to run off with him myself, if he had been so inclined. But he preferred Helen, which also seemed plausible to me. She is very beautiful and carries a melancholy around with her that is quite disarming. If I were partial to females, I would certainly be drawn to her. But, in truth, of all the women I have known, I am most intrigued by the witch, Cassandra. She is not a beauty, although she is pretty, and I believe there is a nice body hidden beneath all those silks that she wears, but it is not her physical appearance that attracts me—it is her mind. She played me for a fool, something that no other person has ever done. And I admire her for that. I am sorry that we were not able to spend more time together. Now that I know her for what she is, I believe we could have been good companions, perhaps even friends. There is nobody in this palace that I can count as my intellectual equal. I am surrounded by vain, ignorant people. It would have been nice to have had someone to talk to. But that was not to be. So I remain alone, admired by most, envied by some, and hated by a few.

Most Greeks presume that Helen was taken against her will. If you ask them, they will tell you that Paris saw her, wanted her, and took her. They believe that because that is what they would have done. People like Agamemnon, Achilles, Diomedes, and the rest are used to getting what they want. If they see something they want, they take it. So they presume that all people are like them, and they judge accordingly. Ironically, only Menelaus is silent on the subject. Everybody assumes it is because he is grief-stricken, or ashamed. Menelaus says little, and so most judge him to be a simpleton. I think there is more to him than meets the eye.

While Menelaus has remained mostly silent and calm, Agamemnon has been completely out of control. His great dream of an alliance with the Trojan royal family went down in flames in one night, and he has spent almost every day and night since roaring drunk, railing against everybody and everything. Only that charlatan Calchas has any influence on him. For months prior to his arrival in Mycenae, Calchas had not spoken a word. Now he never shuts up. He is always throwing his hands in the air, rolling his eyes, chanting, and shouting out nonsense that nobody can understand, except perhaps Agamemnon, who leans over close to him and listens intently as he rants. If you ask me, they are a pair of fools, but nobody asks me, and I have learned that it is best to keep one's thoughts to oneself.

Klytemnestra, Nestor, and Menelaus tried to hold the kingdom together until Agamemnon regained his senses, but they were no match for Achilles, and so we go to war.

With all the madness going on, I was relieved to be assigned to accompany Nestor on a 'peace mission' to Troy. My instructions were simple and clear. I was to do all I could to make sure the mission failed. This proved to be much more difficult than I had imagined. Nestor is a skilled negotiator, and Hector, who spoke for King Priam, is a reasonable and just man.

He came down to greet us on the beach, which I thought was a generous gesture. He was accompanied by a large contingent of court officials, none of whom seemed to be happy wading in the sea foam. Hector, however, acted as if we were all on dry land. He plunged knee-high into the surf to help Nestor ashore, and barked out orders to an army of servants who ran into the water and lifted us to dry land where we were loaded onto litters and carried like royalty into the city.

We could see the walls of the city from miles away at sea. At first, it looked like a small bump on the horizon, but it grew and grew until it loomed above us when we stepped ashore. Even from the shoreline, you could see that Nestor had spoken truthfully—the walls could not be scaled.

It was a long march from the shoreline to the base of the walls, and for the last 100 yards or so, anyone approaching would be in the open and exposed to the archers, who were stationed every few feet along the length of the wall. When we finally reached the base of the wall, I dismounted from my litter and walked in its shadow for some time. Hector made no objection to this, even though he knew I was inspecting the strength of the fortification. I walked quite far in one direction, and although I could determine that the wall curved, I could not see its end.

I stopped walking, and Hector, who had been walking silently behind me said, "It goes on in the same way in the other direction. If you continued walking, following the wall around the citadel, the sun would set before you completed your circuit."

He had made his point. The walls were enormously high, and enormously wide. I would soon learn that they were also enormously thick. They could not be scaled, surrounded nor breached. The citadel appeared to be impregnable.

"I am aware," Hector said, "that you are here on behalf of Achilles, and that Achilles seeks war. You must convince him that war would be a grave mistake."

"Ares himself could not convince Achilles that war would be a mistake."

"Even if it cost thousands of lives?"

"He cares nothing for his own life, or the lives of others. He only cares for glory."

"There is no glory in war."

"You would never convince Achilles of that."

"And what about you? What do you think?"

"I am no lover of war, but I am a lover of Achilles. For all his faults—and he has many, I still love him, and will follow where he goes."

"Even if it means his death, and yours?"

"Even so."

We turned and retraced our steps back to the others, who were waiting patiently for our return—they could not proceed without Hector. I refused to get up on the litter, preferring to walk on my own two feet through the gates into the city. I was right to do so. It was only by walking through the gates that I could get a clear idea of their strength, which was impressive. They were ten times the thickness of the walls around Mycenae. It would take a thunderbolt from Zeus to bring them down.

Hector continued to trail me, but he said nothing. He had no need of words. The walls spoke for him. Agamemnon was boasting that he would build a fleet of 1,000 ships, each with 100 men, and these 100,000 Greeks would reduce Troy to rubble. Achilles outdid his boast, claiming he only needed one ship and one man. But I looked at the walls, and I saw only the bones of 100,000 Greeks bleaching on the sand or piled one on top of the other at the base of the wall, while within the walls, the Trojans ate, drank, and laughed at the foolishness of the Greeks.

While the walls were a marvel, what lay beyond them was even more marvelous. I had never seen so many people crowded into one space. We walked down a broad, level avenue between rows and rows of shops crowded with people, all apparently well off, if one can judge by the quality of their garments. We followed this avenue for some time, then made several turnings, but wherever we went, it was the same scene.

"How big is this place?" I asked Nestor, astounded by the magnitude of the city, and the vast numbers of people lining its streets.

"I don't know," he said. "I have never walked the length of it."

"You were right to counsel against war."

"I am happy to hear you say that. Can I count on you to advise Achilles to seek peace?"

"Yes. I will report what I see and what I think, but do not expect him to change his mind. He thinks only of glory."

"Nevertheless. Your voice is welcome."

* * *

We were taken to our quarters in the royal palace, bathed, clothed and fed, and once refreshed, escorted into the Great Hall where we were presented to King Priam and his Queen, Hecuba, along with Hector and his wife, Andromeda. Paris and Helen were absent. I looked in vain for Cassandra, who was neither seen nor spoken of.

Priam was ancient, weak in body and mind. It was evident that Hector was the real power in Troy. Priam was an empty shell, a figurehead, nothing more. Nestor and I paid our respects to Priam, and immediately turned to Hector.

"I am disappointed," Nestor said. "I had hoped to see Paris and Helen this evening."

"They are weary of public events and prefer to remain in the privacy of their own home."

"I understand their reluctance to attend such tedious events as this, but you must realize that their absence feeds the rumor that Helen was abducted and remains a prisoner here in Troy."

"I can assure you, Hector responded, "that Helen was not abducted, and is content here in Troy. She has no desire to return to Greece."

"I am sorry, Hector," I said, "but you cannot assure us. Only Helen can do that."

Hector's face reddened, and he shouted, "WHAT!" so loudly that a hush fell over the entire hall, and all eyes turned to Hector and me. He inched so close to me that our noses almost touched, and I could feel the heat of his breath upon my face.

"You dare to challenge my word!? He whispered. "I warn you Patroclos, no man calls me a liar and lives long after—not even a coward like you who hides behind the shield of his lover, Achilles."

You might think that I would have been offended by his words, but I was not. I had heard them many times before. I replied calmly, "I meant no offense Hector," I said. "I only meant to point out that we cannot go home to Greece without speaking to Helen. As Nestor said, if we return home without having heard from her own lips what you have said—which, by the way, I believe to be true—we will not be believed. We will be ridiculed, and lucky to escape with our lives. I will surely have need of Achilles' protection then, if he will offer it to such a worthless envoy as I will have proven to be."

Hector accepted my explanation as an apology, saving him from the need to dismember me right there in front of everybody. Nestor took advantage of the moment and urged Hector to not let personal feeling interfere with the larger issue. "If we three cannot find peace, then there is no hope for peace between Troy and Greece," he said. Then he added, "I have a personal message for Helen from her husband, King Menelaus of Sparta. I have promised the King that I will deliver it to her."

"Tell it to me," Hector said. "I will deliver it to her."

"That cannot be; I have given my word that I will deliver it directly to her ears, and her ears only."

"I will inform her. But you must understand, the decision whether to hear your message or not will be hers, and hers alone."

"I have your word on this?"

"I have said so."

"Then I will be patient and await the Queen's answer." With that Hector left us.

"Do you think he will deliver your message?"

"I believe he is a man of honor."

"We shall see. In the meantime, what do you suggest we do?"

"I have a full agenda of meetings with Trojan leaders to discuss reparations. Their Prince has walked off with our Queen. There is no excuse for it—not even if Helen went off voluntarily. It is still a major breach of all of the rules of hospitality. They will have to pay for their Prince's transgression."

"What shall I do while you are negotiating?"

"Go out. Mix. Mingle with the people. Try to find out what the common people think of all of this."

So. for the next fortnight, while Nestor sat in meetings listening to bureaucrats and merchants talk about trade, tonnage, concessions, goods, and a hundred other things I have absolutely no interest in, I wandered the city, from one wine shop to the next, having a very good time for myself.

It didn't take long for me to find a community of like-minded men who quickly adopted me into their group and made a great fuss over me. My reputation had preceded me. It seems everybody had heard of Patroclos, the lover of the great hero Achilles. I was invited everywhere, and never had to pay for anything. Men flocked to me, anxious to see me, speak to me, and touch my garment. I had never had so much attention, and I must admit I enjoyed it, at least for as long as it took me to realize that it was not me they were interested in. It was Achilles. I was besieged with questions about Achilles. "Is he really as beautiful as they say...What is he like in bed? Is it true that he has an enormous penis? And so on, with one ridiculous question after another until I could stand it no longer.

I retreated to my rooms in the palace, refused invitations, and sulked. I had fallen in love with Achilles years ago, and for some time he returned my affection, but lately, his attention was wavering, and I was beginning to doubt that I still had a hold on his heart. How ironic that I should be esteemed in Troy for something so fleeting as a man's affection. No man is true forever. It is not in their nature. Some say that Odysseus is such a man, but I doubt that even he could resist the allure of a younger companion. Let Penelope bear children, grow old and fat, and then judge Odysseus, but not until then.

I was in this sour state when Nestor approached me with news. "Helen has agreed to meet with me," he said, smiling broadly and evidently well pleased with himself.

"And me?" I asked. "Will she meet with me also?"

"No. I am afraid not. She only agreed to meet with me to hear Menelaus' message, and that is private."

"I see," I groused.

"You are in a sour mood. Is there a problem?"

"I am tired of this place. I am of no use here, and I long to return to Greece."

"I am surprised to hear that. From all that I have been told, you have been well treated here."

"Do you have spies everywhere?"

"Not in your heart Patroclos. What is it that has affected you so?"

"I have made many acquaintances here, but no friends, save one. I find these people shallow, and false. And I am tired of making meaningless conversation at endless parties."

"Yes, treating with people you dislike is onerous, but it is necessary if we are to gain useful information. Have your 'meaningless conversations' turned up anything of strategic importance?"

"Only that most Trojans call Queen Helen the 'Greek Whore,' and they have no desire to go to war to protect her from whatever punishment her husband might impose."

"I have heard the same sentiment from most of the merchant class as well," Nestor said. "It seems that the only person who is willing to go to war over Helen is Hector."

"And Achilles...When do you meet with Helen?"

"Tomorrow."

* * *

Nestor came to my quarters looking as sullen as I had looked the day before.

"I take it that your meeting with the Queen did not go well."

"It did not go as I hoped it would, but my hopes were probably too high anyway."

"What did she say?"

"I cannot tell you."

"What do you mean, you cannot tell me?"

"It is between her and Menelaus. You know I have been pledged to silence."

"Can you tell me if she is willing to return to Greece?"

"Under no circumstances."

"Then we will have war."

"I believe you are right. Hector will not force her to return against her will. And that means our goals here have changed."

"What do you mean?"

"We are no longer negotiators. We are spies."

"You are already a spy."

"Yes, and now you must be also."

"Me? I know nothing about spying—except that they are not well treated if they are discovered. "

"Don't worry. You will not be discovered."

"What must I do?"

"Nothing much. You mentioned a friend. Who is this person?"

"A young man. He dotes on me and follows me everywhere. He says he is of age, but I think that he is still in his teens. He claims to be an artist of some sort."

"His name?"

"Sinon."

"He loves you?"

"He says he does, but I think he hates Troy more than he loves me."

"Why?"

"He says the high priests had his mother stoned to death for blasphemy. He has vowed revenge."

"He sounds perfect. Can you send him to me? Will he do my bidding?"

"If I ask him to."

"Then do so. This Sinon may prove useful. There, now, how does it feel to be a spy?"

* * *

We returned to Greece to find more dissension and confusion that we had left behind. Calchas has increased his hold over Agamemnon, who had fallen into a kind of madness, and would do nothing without the charlatan's approval. Achilles told me that Calchas had prophesized a great victory for Greece, but only if Odysseus joined the coalition of forces being gathered in Mycenae, and consequently, Agamemnon had become obsessed with gaining Odysseus' support.

However, Odysseus had, so far, resisted the King's requests to come to Mycenae. So, Agamemnon has decided to take the highly unusual step of going to *him!* Achilles guesses that this decision, like all others, came not from the King's mind, but from Calchas'.

Poor Nestor! I don't know how the old man does it. We had not been in Mycenae for a week before Agamemnon had him up and moving again. This time to Ithaka! At least Troy was civilized. We slept in a palace and ate well. God knows where he will sleep, or what he will find to eat on that barren island. But Agamemnon decrees, and Nestor must obey. The King may be mad, but he is still the King.

There is one positive note. With Agamemnon gone to Ithaka, his brother Menelaus has taken charge of the kingdom, and with it the army, which has quickly grown into a sizable force. It seems that no one wants to go to war over Helen, but everyone wants to go to war. Men from all the provinces are flocking to Mycenae, anxious to test their strength against the Trojans. Poor fools. They think it will be all glory. They haven't seen the walls of Troy. They will waste their strength, and probably their lives in a useless attempt to bring those walls down.

Menelaus has proven to be an able leader. He may not be much of a husband, but he is an excellent general. He has the troops organized, and has imposed a Spartan training regimen, so at least when they face the Trojans, the recruits will be fit and disciplined. Achilles and his men do not take part in the training, which is just as well. He has no restraint. He knows only one way to fight, and that is to the death. If he were to join the drills, he would decimate the force before it ever got to Troy.

Agamemnon and Nestor returned from Ithaka yesterday, Agamemnon is in rare good spirits, and Nestor remains his usual dour self. It seems that somehow or other, they got Odysseus to agree to join with them. Most of the army is here. Only the Cretans and the Ithakans are absent, and the Cretans are only days away. We are waiting for Odysseus. And then it is on to Troy.

* * * *

Helen

They are coming. They are finally coming. It's been more than a year, but the waiting is over. The anxiety, the fear, the rumors, it is all over. They are coming. I can see their sails on the horizon—hundreds and hundreds of them, like black ants crawling along Earth's rim. I have sacrificed to Poseidon, the Earth Shaker, asking him to open the sea and swallow them whole, even Menelaus, who has done me no harm, even he must die. Why should they come here? Why can they not leave us alone? What is it to them that Paris and I love each other? How does our love hurt them? Is love such a crime that it should stir an entire nation to war?

For months, Paris and I have had to endure the scorn of the entire Trojan nation. We have borne up under endless insults—crude, ugly words shouted at us as we passed the common people in the street, and snide, nasty whispers when we mingled with people of our own station. We have been spat at, cursed at, and humiliated. We have had to endure all this only because we love each other. That is our only crime, and the one person with a right to bear us ill will, Menelaus, wishes us well. So what right do these others have to mock and abuse us? And why such outrage from these Greeks who take women, use them, and discard them as the mood moves them?

They say they come to protect their honor. What honor? Whose honor? What honor does the drunken King, Agamemnon, claim? Or the prideful Achilles? Does the brutish Ajax, or the blood-mad Diomedes have any honor to protect? There is not a man among all those Greeks in all those ships, save one, who has any claim to honor.

Hector came to us this morning and bade us accompany him and the King to the walls. "The Greek fleet approaches, and the people need to see us," he said. I did not want to go. I did not think I could bear the insults and the humiliation. For the past two months Paris and I have been living in a villa outside the walls, away from any people other than our servants. It is beautiful, bright and airy, with ponds and streams, arbors, gardens, fields of flowers, and colorful birds that I had never seen before. For the past two months, I have been happy, happier than I have ever been in my life, and now I was being asked to go and face my shame once again. I protested to Paris, but he reminded me that it was Hector who protected us, he who found us this bower, and to him we owed much. "If he asks," Paris said, "we must comply." I knew he was right, but I was not happy.

We left our paradise and joined the royal family in the palace courtyard. King Priam, Hector, and Paris lead the way on foot. Queen Hecuba, Hector's wife, Andromeda, and I followed in covered litters. Court officials and other nobles walked behind, led by Aenaes. I looked for Cassandra, but she was nowhere to be seen. When the King exited the palace grounds, he was greeted by hundreds of people lining the streets, cheering wildly. I listened carefully, but I could detect no falling off when Paris appeared. I dreaded the moment that my litter would leave the courtyard and enter the streets. I thanked the gods that it was covered, and no one would see me weep when they heaped their scorn on me. Imagine my amazement when, instead of jeers, I heard cheers. I could not fathom it. What could account for this change of heart?

The cheering continued as we stepped down from the litters and climbed the steps to the top of the wall. The view from the walls always amazed me. In land–locked Sparta, I never saw the sea. I had never imagined it could be so immense, and so beautiful. But today, its beauty was marred by the appearance of the Greek fleet.

I watched them come, closer and closer, until I could read the insignias on the sails—the lion of Agamemnon, the Cretan bull, the bold, red Lambda Λ of the Spartans, and the fierce black sails of Achilles and his Myrmidons. Hector came close and asked me to tell him which ships belonged to which king. I did as he asked, naming all the ships I knew.

"Let them come," he said. "Their bodies will pile up under these walls. The greatest threat we face is the smell that will rise from their rotting bodies."

"How is it," I asked, "that the people cheer me now, when for months they have shown me nothing but anger and hatred?"

"You can thank the Greeks for that," he answered. "The people may still think you a whore, but you are *our* whore, and they will not let these arrogant, barbaric Greeks take you from us."

I laughed for the first time in many days. "It is a strange way to be loved," I said, "but I am happy for it."

"Whose ship is that?" he suddenly asked, indicating a fierce-looking ship, its prow covered with black hair and fronted with enormous tusks.

"I do not know," I answered. "I have never seen it before."

"It has an ominous look to it," Hector mused.

"Wait," I said. "I think that is an olive tree on the sail."

"What does that tell you?"

"The olive tree is sacred to Athena, and Athena is Odysseus' protectress. He is her favorite."

"I have heard of Odysseus. Cassandra speaks well of him. He is reputed to be wise."

"He is the best of all of the Greeks. I am sorry to see him here."

"Because?"

"Because he is married to my childhood friend, Penelope, and has a young son at home. I had hoped he would have remained there with them—and because he *is* wise and will find a way to bring these walls down."

* * * *

END OF PART ONE

THE DOGS OF WAR

The Wall

Lipos tilted his head to the side and whispered, "Why are we doing this?" Illotos, who was standing next to him in formation, answered, "Agamemnon wants to test their defenses."

"Why doesn't he just ask Nestor? He has been there. He knows their strengths inside and out. I have been told that he has a map of the entire city and the fortifications."

"You are right, Lipos," said Snake, who was standing next in line after Illotos. "This has nothing to do with the Trojans. It is all about us Greeks. All these heroes you see here came for fame and glory, and what have they been doing for the past month? Building fences and digging shit-holes. The Mycenaeans held a meeting two nights ago and told the drunken King that if they weren't going to fight, then they were going home. They had hoped to feed their lust on Trojan women, but there are no women here, just some stray goats."

Lipos laughed loudly, "Yes," he roared, "and they are very hard to hold on to."

Lipos' comment caused a ripple of laughter all along the line, and that brought the wrath of Kretin down on him.

The red-faced sergeant went nose-to-nose with Lipos and shouted, "***This is no tavern brawl, you loudmouthed jackass! In a few minutes, Trojan archers will be using your fat ass for target practice. Let's see how funny you think that is! Now, straighten this line, and shut up—ALL OF YOU!***"

There was a rustle and clink of movement as the men straightened up in response to Kretin's command. Odysseus, who had been standing aside, suppressed a grin, and moved closer to Kretin.

"How are they?" he asked.

"They are ready," Kretin answered. "They will make you proud."

"It is not my pride that concerns me," Odysseus responded, "It is their lives."

Kretin was silent for some time before responding. "This is madness," he murmured through clenched teeth, so that only Odysseus could hear.

Odysseus nodded in agreement. "Take them only until you enter range of the Trojan archers. There is no need to get to the wall. Agamemnon hopes to draw out the Trojans. If he does, then our task is to protect his flank. It is not to throw ourselves against the wall, or die under a hail of Trojan arrows."

"Understood."

"The two men watched as the rest of the Greeks assembled for battle. They were on the left wing, Agamemnon and his large contingent of Mycenaeans and other mainland Greeks held the center; Menelaus and his Spartans were on the right. Diomedes, leader of the Argive forces, was in reserve.

"Where is Achilles?" Kretin asked.

"In his tent. He said if he could not lead, he would not follow."

Kretin did not respond to Odysseus, but instead drew his attention to the Greek forces. "The Spartans will do well," he said, "but the center looks ragged."

Agamemnon's troops, drawn from all over Greece, lacked training and homogeneity. The force had been thrown together rapidly with little consideration for the origins of the men. They were organized in units on a first-come, first-assigned basis, and as a result, men from different cities and regions were lumped together. The men spoke different dialects, and in many cases, couldn't understand each other or their commanding officers. Many men came from towns that held long-standing grudges against each other. The men were as likely to fight against each other as they were to fight against the Trojans.

Their disorganization was evident to the highly efficient, Trojan-trained, Kretin. "Agamemnon better hope that he is not successful in drawing out the Trojans," he observed. "Those men will run."

"We'll soon find out," Odysseus said. "That is the signal to begin."

Agamemnon's chariot rolled to the front of the Greek line and began a slow progress toward the walls. Odysseus moved in front of his men and surveyed them as they stood at attention. He had spent a lot of money on arms and armor, and his troops looked resplendent in their plumed helmets, brightly burnished bronze armor, and their round olive-tree decorated shields.

"Well," he said. "You look like soldiers. Let's see how you fight."

* * *

The Ithakans held their formation as they marched steadily forward. Illotos was nervous; he felt his hands shaking and hoped the others would not notice. No one spoke. The closer they got to the wall, the higher and more threatening it looked. He could see the archers lining the wall. *What are they waiting for?* He thought. And no sooner had he thought it, then the first arrow thumped into the shield of a man two or three places away from him. The line wavered but did not stop. There was a strange, almost musical sound as a thousand bowstrings released a thousand arrows at the same time. Illotos looked up at a sky darkened by a thousand missiles, all, he was convinced, aimed at him.

He heard the order barked by Kretin, ***"TURTLE! TURTLE!"*** and reacted immediately, instinctively, just as he had been trained—down on one knee, behind his shield, his spear propped against the ground pointing out. He felt the comforting presence of the man in the row behind him pressing down on him, and knew that his shield, too, was raised overhead, and his spear also pointed out. He also knew, because he watched during the drills, that the entire Ithakan army now resembled a group of armored turtles with porcupine bristles.

The defense was effective, but frightening. Arrows thudded and thumped into shields and glanced off armor. On occasion, one found its way through the protective cover and struck a human target, prompting an immediate ***"Tighten up, you lazy bastards. Tighten up!"*** from Kretin, and everyone crouched a little lower in their shells.

The barrage continued unabated for what seemed to be hours but was probably only minutes. "How many arrows do those bastards have?" Lipos muttered as much to himself as to anyone else. "Enough to kill us all ten times over," Illotos answered. "They have had a year to prepare for this."

Their conversation was cut short by another order from Kretin. ***"TURTLE BACK!"*** They began a slow, painful crawl backwards, holding their shields aloft, and maintaining their cramped position. The arrows continued to fall, but with each backward step, fewer and fewer reached their target, until, finally, they were out of range.

Another order from Kretin, and the men stood and stretched their aching limbs. They looked around. The ground was covered with arrows, but aside from a few flesh wounds, they had all survived! They could see the men on the walls shaking their fists, shouting obscenities, daring them to come back, and calling them cowards. A few of the men responded by waving their spears and daring the archers to come down off the walls, but a stern look from Kretin put a quick end to it.

The situation to their right, in the center of the line, was far different. When the first few arrows fell, Agamemnon began a wild charge aimed at the massive front gate. His troops followed, and following the example of the King, raced ahead without order or discipline. They were met with a barrage of arrows that decimated the ranks, stopping the charge dead in its tracks. A second barrage was even more deadly as the stunned and confused troops were cut down where they stood. For a moment, the battlefield seemed to be a painting as the Greeks, frozen with fear and lacking leadership, stood motionless in the field. Then, one by one, they turned and ran, dropping their shields and lances along the way.

Agamemnon and what remained of his Royal Guard were abandoned as the huge gates swung open and Trojan charioteers, led by Hector, poured out, and raced toward the King, who stood almost alone and undefended in the middle of the field.

Kretin barked, ***"WHEEL RIGHT! QUICK MARCH!"*** and the men turned and, with Odysseus in the lead, ran to Agamemnon's defense. Menelaus, on Agamemnon's right flank, saw the same thing that Odysseus did and reacted in the same way. It was a race to see who would get to Agamemnon first, the Trojans or the Greeks. The Trojans had the advantage of being mounted and going downhill, but they slowed to slaughter the wounded and fleeing Greeks. Only Hector ignored the opportunity to take part in the carnage, and, instead, went straight for Agamemnon, who was standing in the middle of the battlefield, surrounded by his Royal Guard.

When Hector reached the King, he descended from his chariot and approached on foot. Some of Agamemnon's Royal

Guard fled when they saw him approach. The few who remained fought bravely, but only managed to slow him down. He cut them down as easily as one swats flies on a summer day. He loomed up in front of Agamemnon, who stood wide-eyed with fear, and watched as Hector raised his spear and prepared to send him to Hades.

Hector hurled his spear, which no doubt would have ended Agamemnon's life, had Illotos' shield not intervened. Illotos, being the fastest of the Ithakans, reached Agamemnon before the others, but he had only just barely made it in time. He threw himself headfirst between Hector and the King, and extending his left arm, used his shield to knock Hector's spear aside. But the act of saving Agamemnon's life put his own in jeopardy.

He landed face down on the ground, open to attack. Hector drew his sword, and for a moment, hesitated, undecided on whether to kill Illotos first or Agamemnon. But, for a second time, he was denied. Odysseus and the bulk of the Ithakans had arrived and placed themselves between Hector and his prey. Illotos scrambled to his feet and took his place beside Odysseus. The Trojans rallied to Hector's side. The two armies faced each other only a few yards apart. A battle between the two forces seemed imminent. But Hector surveying the scene, saw Diomedes and his army racing to join the battle, and the Spartans moving in on his flank. He decided he didn't like the odds. He saluted Odysseus and left the field. Odysseus was not anxious to lead his men into a hail of arrows, so he let Hector go unchallenged. Diomedes, on the other hand, raced past Odysseus in vain pursuit of

Hector and the Trojans who were already dissolving behind the quickly closing gate. Diomedes was standing in front of the gate when the arrows came. They thudded into his shield and bounced off his armor. One, finding an unguarded spot, grazed his thigh. His men faltered, and then turned and ran until they were out of the range of the Trojan archers.

Diomedes stood for a moment, cursing the Trojans and daring them to come out from behind the wall and fight, seemingly oblivious to the arrows falling all around him. Eventually, he turned and walked away, cursing and bleeding, back to the Greek camp.

* * * *

Illotos! Illotos!

The wine was flowing freely in the Ithakan camp. The men were feeling very good about themselves. They had not only survived their first encounter with the enemy, but they had earned praise from Kretin and Odysseus. They had not actually fought the enemy, but they had met them with determination and discipline. They had gone toe to toe with the Trojans, and the Trojans had turned away. Lipos and some of the others remembered the sneers and jokes that they had endured from the Mycenaeans when they first entered the palace grounds months earlier, and they took particular glee in knowing that they had stood their ground, while the Mycenaeans had run.

And they had their own hero to toast. The name *ILLOTOS* echoed through the camp over and over, again and again. Illotos was toasted, hoisted on Lipos' shoulders, and paraded around the camp, not once, but several times. The Ithakans could be heard throughout the Greek camp and beyond the walls in Troy.

Illotos sat atop Lipos' shoulders smiling broadly, as happy as he had been when he had defeated Achilles and won the laurel in Mycenae, and almost as happy as he had been when he realized that Demia loved him as much as he loved her. He accepted the men's praise with a grace that was not feigned, and never refused to drink from a flagon or cup when it was offered, no matter who offered it, even the most common soldier.

"Illotos is a good man, a natural leader," Kretin said, observing his demeanor. "The men love him."

"Yes," Odysseus answered, "and that is both good and bad. Praise is like wine, a good thing in moderation, but too much can addle your wits. Some men, once they have tasted fame, cannot do without it. They become reckless and cannot be trusted with leadership. Illotos is young. It remains to be seen what will become of him."

Their conversation was interrupted by Lipos, who deposited a very drunk Illotos at their feet. Illotos lay where Lipos had dropped him.

"Is he conscious?" Kretin asked, but Lipos merely burped and turned away, apparently no less drunk than Illotos.

"They'll be in no shape to fight tomorrow," Kretin said.

Odysseus laughed. "They'll be lucky if they'll be able to stand up tomorrow," he said.

"Or today," Kretin added, looking down at the still prostrate Illotos, who returned Kretin's icy stare with a grin.

"You are drunk, soldier," Kretin said.

"Yesh I am," Illotos responded, still grinning.

"Yes I am, SIR!" Kretin shouted back at him.

Kretin's reprimand shocked Illotos into something close to sobriety. He struggled to pull himself to his feet and give Kretin a proper military salute, while trying unsuccessfully to keep from weaving back and forth.

Illotos was confused. Moments ago, he had been receiving smiles, slaps on the back, and flagons of wine, but now he was facing the stern-looking Kretin, and a frowning Odysseus. He struggled to get control of his thinking, but everything was spinning crazily out of control, including the room. He knew that these two men—Odysseus and Kretin— were unhappy with him, that somehow he had displeased them, and this bothered him, for he loved and admired them, but he could not control himself enough to be able to do or say anything.

If only the room would stop spinning—

"Look out!" Odysseus shouted, and both he and Kretin jumped backwards, just in time to avoid getting spattered with vomit.

Illotos was in misery, sick and ashamed. Vomiting had the strange effect of clearing his head, at least temporarily. He was very quickly sick again.

"You two," Kretin barked at two soldiers who had stopped to watch what was going on. "Take this man to his quarters—and treat him well. He has earned your respect this day."

Odysseus smiled as he watched the two men carry Illotos away. "Poor Illotos," he said, "he will wish he had died at the hands of Hector before this night is over."

Illotos' 'quarters' consisted of a blanket spread out over some hay. He had a smaller blanket that he had rolled into a pillow, and a quilt that Demia had made for him. It was stuffed with lamb's wool and made of fine cotton, cunningly embroidered with scenes of Ithaka. He shared space inside a tent with three other junior officers. Men like Lipos and Snake slept in the open on the ground, huddled around a fire, and wrapped in a single, thin calfskin coverlet, effective against rain, but not cold.

The two men who had carried Illotos to his tent had done nothing more than drop him onto the ground, which is where Lipos and Snake found him when they realized he was gone. They picked him up, stripped his soiled garments, washed him down, placed him in his bed, and covered him with Demia's quilt. They took turns sitting by his side and caring for him until dawn.

* * * *

Hector! Hector!

While the Ithakans were celebrating outside the walls, the Trojans were celebrating inside. There were impromptu parades, street festivals, and a riot of singing and shouting that carried from the streets into the palace where the royal family and other Trojan leaders had gathered to celebrate Hector's victory.

HECTOR! HECTOR! was chanted repeatedly by a large crowd that had gathered outside the palace, demanding to see their hero.

The celebration inside was more restrained, but no less joyous. After a year of tragedy and trepidation, the action was a relief, and the fact that it resulted in a victory made it even better.

King Priam and Queen Hecuba sat at the head of the banquet table, but Hector was the real power in the room and the center of most of the attention. Paris sat next to him, and Aeneas next to him. The three men smiled only occasionally, and accepted praise with restraint.

Helen sat next to Hector's wife, Andromeda, who spoke to her rarely, and then coldly. Helen may have been accepted by the common people, but Andromeda and the rest of her class were not so forgiving. It would be a long, painful evening for

Helen, who maintained her dignity and composure by looking across the table at her husband, and taking pleasure in the fact that he, at least, had been fully embraced by his old friends and companions. She would never cease to feel guilty about what she had done, even though she would not have undone it for all the riches in the world.

"I saw your husband on the field," said Andromeda in a voice intended only for Helen's ears, but loud enough to be heard by those sitting close by.

"You are mistaken, my Lady, Helen answered. "My husband was not on the field today."

"I was speaking of Menelaus."

"Then you are mistaken again. My husband is Paris."

"I thought he looked quite impressive."

"I agree. Paris is very impressive."

"I was referring to Menelaus."

"I am surprised you are so taken with the Greek. I thought Hector was much his superior, but if you are so enchanted with Menelaus, I could probably arrange an introduction for you."

Andromeda turned from Helen without another word.

"They are calling for you, my dear," she said to Hector. "Show yourself to them."

"It would not be right," Hector responded. "I am not the king. It is Priam's place to appear before the people."

"But it is not Priam the people call for. It was not Priam who led the men out of the gate and drove the Greeks away from the walls. It was you. The people know that Priam is just a shadow. You are true King of Troy. It is time you took your rightful place."

"Be quiet, Andromeda. You don't know what you say. My rightful place is at the right hand of my father. It is an offense to put myself forward before my time."

"Priam will not be offended," she scoffed. "He is beyond knowing offense."

"It is not Priam that I would offend nor is it he that I fear. It is Zeus, the Father God whose wrath I fear, and you would be well to fear it too. His anger falls not only on those who act against their parents, but also those who speak against them."

Andromeda, chastened, lowered her eyes, and remained silent. Hector turned to Paris and Aeneas, who were close enough to hear the exchange.

"Andromeda is right in one regard," Aeneas whispered to Hector, "the people are calling for you, and they have to be satisfied."

"Perhaps," Paris said," You could go with Priam, instead of in his place?"

"Good idea," Aeneas exclaimed, "and let's make it one better. Why don't we all—you, me, Paris, and Priam—show ourselves to the crowd? In that way. They will get to see their hero, and also see that the royal family is unified."

"I don't think that will offend Zeus, do you brother?" Paris chided. "Piety is a good thing, but sometimes I think you overdo it. You are far too serious."

"And you are far too frivolous," Hector responded.

The three men rose, gathered up Priam, stepped out on to the balcony, and were greeted with a roar like none other ever heard in Troy.

"The people love you, brother," Paris shouted above the clamor of thousands of voices.

"They love victory," Hector responded. "But this war is not over. It is too soon to celebrate."

"Oh no," Paris said, clutching at his chest and pretending to be shocked, "Have we offended one of the gods?"

"Do not mock him," Aeneas interjected. "Be thankful, he is here to lead in your father's place."

"You are right. He is a good man, and I love him, but can we not be happy for one night at least?"

At that point, a servant came carrying Hector's son, Astyanax. Hector lifted the child over his head and showed him to the crowd, throwing them into a frenzy of cheers and shouts.

After several moments, Hector lowed Astyanax, and the group left the balcony. The crowd began to disperse, some to their homes, but most to the taverns where they continued their celebrations into the early morning hours.

After the riotous atmosphere outside the palace, the celebration inside seemed reserved. Not that people weren't smiling and happy—they were, exceedingly so. And they drank as much as the commoners; however, they were not so loud, and they tended to drift off in couples, so the party and the party goers thought themselves more sophisticated than the rabble in the streets.

Given a reprieve from public duties, and with fewer people demanding to clap him on the back and congratulate him, Hector took an opportunity to speak with Aeneas and Paris about the battle.

"Did you see anything that surprised you?" He asked Aeneas, who had been stationed on the ramparts where he could see the entire field of battle and assess the combatants.

"Yes," Aeneas answered. "The Ithakans. When I saw them in Mycenae, they were a band of ragamuffins, better suited to a bar brawl then a battlefield.

"I can assure you they did not look like an undisciplined band of hooligans when I saw them. Their leader, Odysseus, looks like a formidable enemy."

"Helen speaks highly of him," Paris added. "She says that he is the most noble of all the Greeks, but also the most cunning. She admires him, but she also fears him."

"I was also surprised by the ferocity of Diomedes," Aeneas said. "In Mycenae, they speak of his brutality. But he is no mere brute; he is a mad man. I have seen men like him in battle. When the blood lust is upon them, they fight without fear and without mercy. Pray that he never enters these walls."

"What did you think of Menelaus and his Spartans?"

"As expected. Disciplined. Formidable."

"I thought your archers were undisciplined," Hector said to Paris. "They wasted far too many shafts on targets that were out of range. Speak to them."

"I will. You can be sure they will hear from me."

"So much for the past," Aeneas said. "What are your plans for the future?"

"Sit tight. Preserve our water. Preserve our arrows. I think the Greeks have learned the strength of our walls. If they are wise, they will go home, but they are not wise. They will stay and try to find another way."

"Our villages and farms are unprotected," Aeneas said.

"You will have to call back troops from the frontier."

"That will leave our border open to invasion," Aeneas said.

"We must protect the homeland first. After we have driven these Greeks off, we can take care of the frontier."

"How long do you think they can maintain the siege?"

"Only as long as they have provisions. Our fleet must keep them contained in the harbor."

"Our ships are no match for their triremes," Paris noted.

"But they are warships, not cargo ships. They carry men, not provisions. Their cargo ships are easy targets if they are not defended by triremes, and if the Greeks pull their men off the barricade to man them, then they will not have enough men left to defend themselves."

"So," Aeneas said, "They must choose which to defend."

"Yes," Hector responded. "Just as we must choose between our frontier and our homeland, the Greeks must choose between their ships and their barricade.

"There is something else. I have a spy in the Greek camp, a certain young man, Sinon, who is friendly with Achilles' lover Patroclos. I do not care much for him, but he is useful. He reports that there is great dissension in the Greek ranks. Achilles refuses to fight under Agamemnon's command, and all the Greeks are tired of digging. They want to fight or go home. I think we should be ready to seize upon any opportunity their dissension affords us."

"Are you suggesting that we attack?" Paris asked.

"No. I am saying that we should be prepared to attack if the opportunity presents itself."

"We will be ready," Aeneas said.

* * * *

In the Tent of Achilles

Diomedes was out of control. ***"He ran!. He ran!"*** he shouted. He had already broken several chairs, smashed in the face of one servant and sent the remaining two running for their lives. Ajax watched him wide-eyed, Achilles watched in amusement, and Patroclos with disgust.

"To be precise," Patroclos said dryly, "the Myrmidons ran. Agamemnon stayed."

"***Frozen in fear!***" Diomedes shouted. "He never even raised his sword. One look at Hector and he turned into stone! If it weren't for that Ithakan throwing himself in front of Hector's spear, we would be putting Agamemnon's body on the funeral pyre, and I, for one, would gladly set it aflame."

"Yes," Patroclos remarked with a glance in Achille's direction, "that was quite a feat. I'm not sure that I could have done it."

"It wasn't so noteworthy," Achilles said. "It would have been better if he had remained on his feet and challenged Hector."

"I wish you had been there," Diomedes continued. "Things would have been a lot different."

Diomedes had inadvertently entered dangerous territory. Agamemnon had offered the left flank to Achilles, but he had turned it down, claiming he, not Agamemnon, should lead the Greeks into battle. This was completely unreasonable since Agamemnon, not Achilles, was the King. However, reason rarely entered into anything Achilles did. Pride, reputation, glory, these were the things that motivated him, and in this case, they led him to absent himself from the battle, a decision that did not sit well with most of the Greek leaders who felt that, since Achilles was the one who lobbied most strongly in favor of the war, it was wrong of him to sit in his tent while others went out to fight. Diomedes and Ajax remained loyal, but most of the others had turned against him.

"Will you be at the council tomorrow?" Patroclos asked Diomedes, in an attempt to change the subject.

"Yes, Ajax and I will be there. Will you?"

Diomedes' reference to Achilles' absence from the field had soured his mood, so Achilles merely shrugged, but Patroclos answered, "We will be there."

"Good," Diomedes said. "I am anxious to hear Agamemnon's excuse for his cowardice."

"Until tomorrow, then" Patroclos said as he ushered the two men out of the tent.

"Fools!" he muttered after the men had left. Achilles frowned, but said nothing. He had been stung by Diomedes' comment. He knew now that it had been the wrong decision to sit out the battle, but his pride would never let him admit an error.

It was such a sensitive issue with him that even Patroclos didn't dare mention it. But it was too late. The issue had seeped into Achilles' brain and taken refuge there. He had played out the events of the battle over and over until he could recite them, but in his version, he, not Odysseus, confronted Hector. And in his version of events, he defeated Hector in man-to-man combat. There was, in his mind at least, not only the way it should have turned out, but the way it undoubtedly would have turned out if only he had not decided to stay in his tent in protest. He had missed an opportunity for a glorious victory, or a glorious death—either would have been better than the current situation. He didn't however, blame himself for his misfortune, but Patroclos.

"I should never have listened to you," he said, completely out of the blue.

Patroclos, taken back and confused, asked, "Listen to me about what?"

"I let you talk me into staying off the field!"

Patroclos knew that wasn't true, but he and Achilles had been lovers for almost eight years, and in those eight years, he had learned that it was useless to argue with him—far better to simply shut his mouth, bury his head, and take the verbal blows that were sure to follow. Better that than physical blows. The storm would pass. It always did, and when it did Achilles would apologize, ask for forgiveness, and promise never to do it again.

Of course he would do it again. He always did it again. That's who he was. Patroclos often asked himself why he stayed with him. He was vain, arrogant, unfaithful, and a bully. When they had first met eight years earlier, Achilles was already recognized as a great warrior, and Patroclos was a 21-year-old, handsome and accomplished young man, one of the brightest stars in the Greek galaxy. It was inevitable that he should turn up in Achilles' bed. What was remarkable was that, eight years later, he was still there. This was entirely due to his efforts, not Achilles.

Achilles desired him, but he *loved* Achilles. That was always the difference between them, and the fault line in their relationship. Patroclos knew that Achilles did not love him, but he had convinced himself that Achilles needed him, and that was almost the same thing.

Achilles always told everybody that the gods had offered him a choice between a long life and a peaceful death surrounded by friends and family and a short, glorious death in battle, and he had chosen the latter. He told this story so often that every child in Greece could repeat it word-for-word. He was very proud of it. But what he didn't realize was that, in choosing the short, glorious life, he had given up not only years of life, but friends and family as well. He was totally alone—except for Patroclos. He had admirers, sycophants, hangers-on, and lots of enemies, but no friends. Patroclos knew what Achilles did not—that when the moment of his death came, he would be alone, and he would not be greatly mourned. What sustained Patroclos through all the infidelity and abuse was his belief that, somewhere deep inside that pea-sized brain of his, Achilles knew that he had him, and only him—and without him, he would be totally alone.

"It's your fault!" Achilles roared at him, waking him from his reverie. He had been walking around the tent, raging for a while. Patroclos had been self-absorbed and hadn't heard a word.

"What's my fault?" he said irritably, like a man who had been awakened from a deep sleep.

"Everything!" Achilles shouted. "Do you hear that shouting coming from the Ithakan camp? Do you hear it! That's all for some idiot who threw himself in front of a spear instead of taking the opportunity to attack Hector. Those cheers should have been for me. I should have been there, not some nobody!"

"No doubt you are right," Patroclos responded. "It is idiocy to throw yourself in front of a spear. I would never do it. Still, it was very impressive." He paused before completing his thought. He knew he shouldn't say it, but he had been stung, and the impulse to strike back was irresistible. "I believe, "he said with a mischievous smile, "the idiot was Illotos, the same young man that bested you and took the laurel at the games in Mycenae."

Achilles turned purple with rage and ran at Patroclos, sword in hand. He put the sword to Patroclos' throat and spit out through clenched teeth, "If you are so impressed with this Illotos, why don't you seek him out in the Ithakan camp. You seem to be drawn to young men these days."

Patroclos didn't flinch. He was used to Achilles and had grown used to his tantrums.

"I have no interest in Illotos, and you know it," he said calmly, "but what is this about 'young men'?"

"You think I don't know about the boy you have stashed away in your quarters?"

"Sinon? Is that what this is about? You are jealous of Sinon?" Patroclos was delighted. If Achilles were jealous, that meant he cared for him. He laughed so hard he started to cry.

"What is so funny?"

"You. You're right. Sinon is little more than a boy. I am many things, Achilles, but I am no lover of boys. I much prefer men, and you are the greatest of men. Why do you think I put up with you?"

If there was one way to calm the rage of Achilles, it was with flattery, and being referred to as 'the greatest of men' did the trick. Achilles lowered his sword and spoke much more calmly.

"If he is not your lover, why is he staying in your quarters?"

"Nestor uses him as a spy. He is a Trojan, but he loves me, and he hates Troy, so I let him stay in my quarters. It pleases him. He is fashioning a horse for me."

"A horse?"

"Yes, a life-sized, wooden horse. I saw one like it in the entrance hall to the palace in Troy and I admired it. Sinon said it was trash and that he could make one ten times better. So I bade him do it. It keeps him busy and away from me."

"What a waste of time," Achilles said.

****

The Smell of Death

The next day, Nestor met with Aeneas in the shadow of the walls. The old man had to pick his way among the corpses and cover his face to protect himself from the odor of human flesh rotting in the Trojan sun. It would have been a difficult task for a younger man, but Nestor never wavered in his duties.

Aeneas agreed to restrain his bowman so the Greeks could claim their dead from the battlefield. He also agreed to a two-day truce to allow the Greeks to properly honor the dead. He did this partially as a matter of professional courtesy, and partly because, with the wind blowing in off the sea, the smell was already becoming a problem inside the city and was sure to get worse. As a practical matter, the Greeks would have been better off letting the corpses rot where they lay and hope that the lovely sea breezes would carry a deadly pestilence to the citizens of Troy. But to do so would have been considered an offence to the gods, and the Greeks, who feared the gods more than they feared the Trojans, elected to collect their dead and perform the proper funerary rights—besides, Calchas was predicting disaster if they failed to honor the dead.

For the following two days, smoke and the sickly sweet smell of burning flesh rose from a large funeral pyre that had been constructed from driftwood gathered from the length and breadth of the beach. It was under this cloud that the Greeks met in council to determine their next steps.

Agamemnon sat at the head of the council table, flanked by Menelaus and Nestor. The rest of the Greek leaders sat in no particular order, but there was an audible buzz when Achilles and Patroclos entered the room after everybody else had already been seated. Diomedes and Ajax Major moved aside to make room for them at the foot of the table.

Odysseus stayed quiet for most of the meeting, preferring to let the others argue over who was to blame for the debacle at the wall. A few dared to suggest that Achilles was responsible for not showing up, but no one could deny the cowardice of the Myceneans, and Agamemnon's lack of leadership. His more vocal opponents called for him to be driven from the camp in disgrace. In the end, Agamemnon was allowed to keep his title of King, but had to transfer all military operations to his brother, Menelaus. Achilles agreed that he and his Myrmidons would fight alongside Menelaus, but not under his command.

Once that compromise had been agreed upon, Odysseus rose to speak. He began by pointing out that for the past two days, they had scoured the beach for every bit of driftwood they could find and still only had barely enough to build a pyre. Then he reminded them that in all their exploration of the beachfront, they found neither food nor water.

"The only food and water we have is what we brought with us," he said. "One month's supply—that is all we thought we would need. We thought that before one month had passed, we would be in Priam's palace, dining on Trojan lamb and drinking Trojan wine. But the attack on the walls proved otherwise. Not the strength of Ajax, nor the fury of Diomedes, nor the courage of Achilles will bring those walls down. That is evident. So where does that leave us?"

The men stirred in their seats while Odysseus paused to let them think over their options.

Then he began again, and everybody leaned forward to hear what he had to say.

"It is obvious that Hector has neither the need nor the desire to venture further outside the walls than his archers can reach—unless we grow so weak that he sees a chance to be rid of us once and for all—and we *will* grow weak without food and fresh water."

This created a greater stir among the Greek leaders, who began to see where this was going. Some began to speak out, believing that Odysseus was going to urge them to give up the siege.

But he silenced them with a wave of his hand and continued, "We must find fresh supplies before we starve to death and fill the air with the stench of our rotting corpses."

"You have a plan?" Nestor asked with a wry smile.

"I have a plan."

"I thought as much," Nestor said, "Will you share it with us?"

"I will," he said," if you wish to hear it."

Odysseus' plan was simple. The terrain to the south of the city was a flat, rich, agricultural plain. But in anticipation of the Greek attack, the Trojans had harvested whatever crops they could, and burned the fields so they would yield no sustenance for the invaders. And, in addition to offering nothing of value, the open, level field was perfect for cavalry, which the Trojans had, and the Greeks did not.

The land to the south was a marsh formed by the delta of the River Scamander. The water there was brackish and the footing treacherous, but it was here that Odysseus planned to go. He directed that several of the triremes be dismantled and reconstructed as flat-bottomed scows, capable of skimming over the sand bars and marshland that clogged the delta's mouth.

"Beyond the delta," Odysseus said, "the Scamander runs clear and clean. It is too far from the walls of Troy to present a risk from that quarter, and its banks are lined with tall reeds that limit the ability of ground troops to maneuver. Cavalry cannot operate there at all. We go up at night. Two scows with troops, one in the front, the other in the rear. All the other scows go upriver empty and return with fresh water. Small hunting parties can scour the south side of the river in search of game."

"Won't the Trojans try to stop us?" someone asked.

"Perhaps, but if they do, we will deal with them. I have no doubt that if we remain outside of the range of their archers, we are more than a match for them."

* * * *

Up a Lazy River

The next morning the Greeks began dismantling some of their ships. At the same time, they began digging a trench all along the entire beachfront in front of their encampment and using the dirt from the trench to build a defensive wall.

"What in the world are those crazy Greeks doing," Paris asked Aeneas, both of whom were standing on the ramparts watching all the activity taking place on the beach.

"They are building a defensive barricade and, according to Hector's spy, Sinon, using wood from the ships to strengthen it."

"Then they intend to stay?"

"It seems so."

"Their bones will rot on that beach."

"Let us hope so."

* * *

Sinon had done his job, and the Trojans watched passively as the Greeks took first one ship apart and then another and laid the wood down behind the growing sand and dirt barricade. However, they did not see that in the evening, the

Greeks took the wood from the barricade and used it to build the flatboats that Odysseus would need to sail up the Scamander.

It took about a week to get everything ready. As usual, the Greeks fought over who should have the honor of leading the expedition, but eventually they agreed that since it was Odysseus' idea, he should be in charge.

Odysseus waited for a cloudy night with only a small sliver of the moon shining weakly in the western sky before setting out. The barges had to be towed out past the breakers and around the headland before being set free in the calm waters of the Scamander delta. There, the oarsmen took over, and the barges moved silently over the sandbars and through the weed-choked estuary until they found a clear, quick-moving channel of clean water.

Odysseus ordered the barges to stop and begin gathering water in the ewers and urns that they had brought with them. This was a time-consuming process, so he sent armed men to the northern shore to keep a watch for Trojan patrols. He also sent out several small hunting parties to the southern shore to look for game. Bowmen on board the scows took down several seabirds. Fish were plentiful in the river and could be caught with nets thrown over the side.

Odysseus' patrols and scouting parties had encountered no Trojans, but still, he was nervous. It was inconceivable to him that the Trojans would simply abandon such a valuable region. Was it possible that they were so confident in the strength of their walls, that they felt no need to protect the surrounding area? He had to know, so he called Kretin aside and told him to select a few of his best men and scout upriver. He told him to observe, but under no circumstances, engage with any Trojans should he come across them. This was a reconnaissance mission only. It was important that the Trojans remain ignorant of their presence on the river.

Kretin chose only two men, Illotos and Snake. At first, Lipos was enraged that he had not been selected, but when he learned that the mission could involve crawling along on his belly for hours at a time and maintaining complete silence for the entire night, he decided it was all right after all.

Kretin, when he told Odysseus of his choice of men, joked, "Can you imagine Lipos trying to go an entire night without one of his monstrous farts? We'd be discovered in no time."

The three men stripped off their armor, looped a sword over their shoulders and tied a knife to their waists before stepping off the scow into the dense growth of reeds that screened the river from view and immediately sinking knee-deep in mud and water. They cursed, while Lipos, looking on from the deck, tried to hold back his laughter.

Snake, already annoyed in his muddy prison, turned red with anger as Lipos' laughs rang in his ears. "It's a good thing Kretin left that fat pig behind," he whispered to Illotos. "With his weight, he would have sunk up to his neck in this muck."

"And it would take the whole Greek army to pull him out," Illotos responded, earning a laugh from Snake and a growl from Kretin, "Shut up you two," he said. "This is not a picnic you have been invited to."

Illotos and Snake immediately stopped talking and began the difficult and painstaking task of extricating themselves from the marsh. They lifted one leg straight up until it was out of the ooze and then put it down again as far in front of them as they could stretch. Then they lifted the back foot up, turned sideways, and placed it down in front of them. They repeated this process over and over again until, at last, they found solid footing.

The air was still and so humid they struggled to breathe. They walked until they were completely out of the marsh and could sit down and clean themselves. They used leaves to scrap the mud off their legs and their knives to remove the leeches that clung to their legs, but they could do nothing about the mosquitoes that incessantly buzzed around their heads and necks in a blood–induced frenzy.

"Damn!" Illotos exclaimed as one landed in his eye.

"Sshh!" Kretin hissed. "Ignore them."

"Easy for him to say," Snake whispered. "He has no blood."

"He has blood," Illotos whispered back, "But the bugs like it warm, and his is cold."

The men walked on, and the further they got from the river, the less onerous the trek became. A light breeze brought fresh air and drove the mosquitoes away. It wasn't long before the men came to a road. It was wide, and the wagon ruts were deep, so it was apparently well used. Illotos and Snake stayed hidden in the foliage that bordered the road while Kretin scouted the area. He was gone only a short time, and when he returned, he said nothing, but indicated that the two men should follow him as he moved off to the left, a direction, Illotos assumed, that led away from Troy.

They followed the road but avoided walking on it, preferring to keep out of sight by moving through the shrubs and trees that bordered it. They walked for some time without seeing anybody, then they heard the mooing of a cow, and saw an old man directing a pair of cattle by prodding them now and then with a long, thin stick.

Illotos drew his sword, and Snake his knife, but Kretin neither moved, nor gave them any signal to attack. They both were eager to do so, not that they bore the old man any ill will, but they had not eaten any fresh meat since they left Ithaka several months ago, and they had visions of dining on the steaks the cattle would provide.

Their feast would have to wait, Kretin was more interested in where the man was going than in dreaming of an imaginary feast. They waited until the man disappeared beyond a turn in the road and then rose and began to follow him. The man walked leisurely, and the cattle seemed to know where to go without any prodding.

Kretin, Illotos and Snake followed along silently for more than a kilometer, and just when they were starting to think of turning back, their patience was rewarded. Just ahead of them, on a small rise, stood a very large temple, and surrounding the temple a complex of official-looking buildings, and beyond that, a small town surrounded by neatly plowed fields.

They crept up to the temple to get a better look.

"Apollo," Illotos whispered.

Kretin nodded.

Kretin allowed himself a small smile before turning to leave.

"Wait!" Illotos hissed.

A small number of young women had just entered the main hall of the temple and began laying flowers around a large statue of Apollo. They watched for a while as the women worked. Two priests arrived. Then the man with the cattle came into the temple and spoke with the priests.

"What's going on?" Snake asked.

"They are getting ready for a ceremony," Kretin answered.

"The Apollonia!" Illotos explained. "It's a dawn ceremony, performed in honor of the god. They are probably planning it to give thanks for their victory.'

"*SHIT!*" Kretin spit out almost too loudly.

Illotos and Snake looked at him in alarm.

"Damn!" he said. "I forgot. We have to get back to the boats. NOW!"

They left the temple area and made their way back to the roadway, but everything had changed from when there were there earlier. The road was filled with people, including a full complement of soldiers.

"Looks like everybody's coming to the party," Snake said. "If we wait, we might get a shot at Hector and Priam."

"If we wait, we'll be dead," Kretin said. "We have to find another way back."

"How about the river?" Illotos asked.

"The river?" Snake exclaimed, "Are you crazy? There's snakes in the river."

"Then you should feel right at home," Illotos quipped.

"It's the river or Hades," Kretin said.

"The river," Snake said.

* * *

Odysseus paced the deck nervously. Kretin should have been back. It would be getting light soon, and the high tide would not last too much longer. If he didn't leave soon, the now-filled, heavy scows would not be able to clear the sand bar at the mouth of the delta. They would be trapped in a closed estuary in full view of the enemy. Odysseus knew they would have to leave, with or without Kretin. And that would mean leaving without Illotos too.

Odysseus understood war. He knew that people died. He had lost family and friends in the never-ending feuds and squabbles that characterized Greek life, but Illotos was special. He had protected him, mentored him, and watched him grow into a man, a man who was now a husband and soon-to-be father. He paced the deck, staring off into the darkness, fearing the rising sun and sinking tide.

He made up his mind. He ordered the other ships to leave. He would stay until the situation was certain. Lipos came to him, frantic.

"Let me put together a search party and look for them," he pleaded, but Odysseus refused.

"Where would you look?" he asked. The entire area was inky black. The sun had not yet risen. "Two steps into that darkness, and you, too, would be lost."

"They probably followed the river upstream," Lipos said. "Can we not at least sail upriver in search of them?"

"No. If they are alive, they will come here. Here is where they will expect to find us, and here is where we will be. I know this is difficult. I too love Illotos, perhaps more than you, but you must put your faith in them. They are tough, resourceful men. If they are alive, they will find their way back here."

At that point the first slight glimmer of light lined the eastern horizon, dispelling some of the deeper shadows, and making the west-flowing Scamander look like a silver ribbon in the darkness.

"*SIRE!*"

Odysseus spun around at the sound of the helmsman's voice and looked upstream at the unlikely sight of three naked men holding onto a log and waving.

* * * *

Ithaka

It had been more than two months since Odysseus and Illotos had set sail for Troy, and Demia's pregnancy was not going well. She had collapsed in the field and been forced to stay in bed—much against her will. Penelope had sent Eurycleia to take care of her, and the kind old lady was sitting by Demia's bedside with a bowl of warm broth, trying in vain to get Demia to sit still.

The room was basic, but pleasant. Demia had scrubbed the place clean, thrown out all the old, broken pieces of furniture, and with the help of Penelope, turned what had been a cluttered and neglected space into a warm and welcoming bedroom for her and Illotos. Penelope had woven a blanket as wedding gift. It was an ingenious piece of work, intricately interwoven with plants, flowers, trees, and if you looked closely, small birds. Demia loved it, as she loved this room and this bed—the bed in which she and Illotos had made love and created the child that she now carried, the bed in which she would bring that child to life.

It was not grand, neither the room nor the bed, but for Demia nothing in the world could compare to it. It comforted her, even as she lay ill, fretting under Eurycleia's watchful eyes.

Charis entered the room and sat by Demia's side. She took the younger girl's hand and held it tightly. A small tear escaped from the corner of her eye.

Demia gasped. "What's wrong? Have you had news? Is it Illotos?!"

"No, no, it is nothing like that. I have had no news."

"What then?"

"It's Eurymachus."

"What has he done now?"

"He was walking up the to the house as brazen as can be, just as if he owned it."

"He will own it if the men don't return soon," Eurycleia croaked without once turning her attention away from Demia.

"That's what he said too—more or less. When I asked what business he had here, he said, 'I have business with the lady of the house and it is no business of yours.' You have no business here," I answered, "and you have been told so before."

"He came closer, and I could smell the wine on his breath. You are drunk," I said. "Go back to your tavern and your whores and leave honest people alone. 'You and that princess think you are so high and mighty,' he said. 'You'll change your tune when my father takes over.'"

"What does he mean?" Demia said angrily, "When his father takes over? Takes over what?"

"Everything," Eurycleia said.

The two women stared at the old lady, waiting for her to explain her words, but she remained silent.

Finally, Demia demanded, "What do you mean, 'everything'?"

"You are not so young that you do not have eyes to see?" the old lady responded. "The field hands and shepherds have left us; the crops are rotting in the fields for lack of picking, and that man's father is the cause of it. He buys off or scares off the help, and when the farm fails, he buys it at a bargain price. He has done it before—with Illotos' father's land, and he plans to do it again with this land."

"I cannot stay here," the girl pleaded. "There is too much to do, and I promised Illotos that I would take care of his property while he is gone. I cannot let him come home and find that I have let the land go to ruin."

"Would you prefer to have him come home and find you and his babe have gone to ruin? The land has been here since long before you and I were born, and it will be here long after we are gone. Do not worry about the land. Worry about yourself and your child."

Tears began to course down Demia's cheeks. "I feel so stupid," she said. "I am useless. Other girls work in the field up until their time. Why can't I? They are right. I am a spoiled, useless brat, good for nothing..."

"Hush! Who says such things?"

"I hear them in the village, talking behind my back. 'Who does she think she is?' they say. 'A princess. And what good is a princess on this rocky isle? Illotos will be sorry he brought her here.'"

"Don't listen to them. They're just a bunch of jealous washerwomen with nothing better to do than talk nonsense all day long. There's more to worry about than that."

"You are right," Demia said between sobs. "I should be thinking of Illotos—two months, and not a word! He might be wounded, or maybe even dead!"

"Do not worry about Illotos. He is with Odysseus, and Odysseus will bring him home. I mean no disrespect to your Illotos. He is a fine man, but there is none like Odysseus."

"Still, he is somewhere far from home, in danger, and all I can think about is myself. I am truly worthless!"

"You are not worthless," Charis said. "You are barely 18, pregnant with your first child, and missing your husband. But you must take care of yourself and your child. Promise me you will."

"Very well. I will stay put. I don't seem to have much choice anyway. But," she said to Eurycleia, "you said, 'there's more to worry about.' What did you mean?"

"Polybus is a drunken fool, but his father, Eurymachus, is a man to be reckoned with, and I have heard that he has sent messengers to Mycenae."

"Ugh!" Charis said. "I despise that man—always leering at Penelope. He makes my skin crawl. If Odysseus were here, he wouldn't come within a mile of her."

"You are right," Eurycleia said, "but Odysseus is not here and so he comes sniffing like a dog hoping to make his mark."

"You said that he sent messengers to Mycenae. What is the significance of that?"

"Mycenae is where the Great King used to rule," the old
lady said.

"I am young," Demia responded with some temper, "But I
am no fool. I know well that the Great King ruled in Mycenae,
and I also know that he is gone to Troy and taken my Illotos
with him..."

"...and we both know," Charis added, "That he no longer
rules there. Klytemnestra now rules the kingdom. What is
your point?"

The old lady continued to tend to Demia, wiping her brow,
and washing her arms with a cooling lotion. She took her
time before answering. And when she did answer, all she said
was, "Lord Odysseus' agreement was with the Great King."

It was enough. Charis gasped. "You think that Polybus
seeks to come to some arrangement with the Queen!"

The old lady said nothing. Demia started to cry. Charis
grew angry, "That bitch!" she hissed. "She will betray
Odysseus just to spite her husband—and she has no love for
you or me."

"Are we are lost, then? Is there no hope for us?"

"Calmly, calmly, my dear," the old lady said. "You must
think only about your child. Odysseus will return and set all
to rights."

"Eurycleia is right," Charis said. "You must take care of
yourself and your babe until Odysseus and Illotos return."

"Let us hope then that they return before it is too late,"
Demia said between tears.

* * * *

The Temple of Apollo

Odysseus returned with four barges loaded with jugs of water and a large assortment of small game that the hunting parties had killed, so for the first time since they arrived in Troy, the Greeks ate fresh meat and drank fresh water. To celebrate the success of the venture, Agamemnon ordered extra wine for the troops, and as they ate and drank, the mood in the camp improved perceptibly.

However, not everybody was happy. Achilles stayed in his tent and refused the meat that was offered to him. Patroclos sat across the table from him eating ravenously.

"This is delicious," he said as he stabbed a piece of rabbit with his knife and brought it to his mouth. "You really should try it."

"I have no appetite for Odysseus' scraps," Achilles responded with some petulance. "It would stick in my throat. I am surprised that you can say you are loyal to me while you flaunt the Ithakan king's triumph in my face."

"I am loyal to you, but I am hungry too, and this is the first meat I have seen in months," Patroclos responded lightheartedly. "How can you say you love me, yet are content to see me starve?"

Achilles threw a cup of wine at Patroclos who ducked and laughed. "You are the only person who can taunt me so, and live to tell about it," Achilles said.

Patroclos was about to respond when Diomedes entered full of excitement. "I have an idea!" he exclaimed.

"An idea," Patroclos murmured, "How extraordinary." Then, in response to Achilles' scowl, said in a loader voice, and with feigned enthusiasm, "What is it? Tell us!"

Diomedes sat down, picked up a piece of rabbit and shoved it into his mouth. He began talking and eating at the same time and doing both so rapidly that neither Patroclos nor Achilles had any idea what he was talking about.

"This must be some idea," Patroclos whispered to Achilles, "He is speaking in the language of the gods."

"Have you been taking lessons from Calchas?" Patroclos asked Diomedes. "We cannot understand a word you are saying." Achilles smiled, even though he disapproved of Patroclos' mockery.

Diomedes, unaware that he was the butt of Patroclos' humor, swallowed hard and began again.

Odysseus brought back food and water," he said, "but he left the greatest prize behind. His scouts reported a large temple complex not much further upriver than where they stopped. According to the scouts, the temple is unguarded— except by priests and priestesses." He emphasized the word 'priestesses' and smiled.

Patroclos, who was in a flippant mood, and could not control himself, said, "Priests and acolytes would be better, but I guess there is no accounting for taste."

* * *

Early that evening, just after sunset, Achilles and Diomedes took one of the barges, outfitted it with a complement of men-at-arms, and had it towed around the headland into the Scamander delta. They rowed upriver in darkness, looking for signs of the temple that Odysseus had discovered. It took longer than they had thought it would, but eventually the temple's arches came into view, outlined against the dark, gray-black moonlit sky.

They moored the barge and marched off in the direction of the temple. Their path intersected the road, which, at that time of night, was completely deserted. They took the road and very quickly reached an open square, lined on three sides with temples. As they were standing there, trying to determine where to strike first, three elderly women appeared, walking casually across the square, their arms full of equipment for the temple. At first, the women did not notice the soldiers standing in the shadows in one corner of the square. When they did, they stopped and stood motionless, staring in fear and disbelief. For a moment, both groups simply looked at each other in silence. Then, simultaneously, the women screamed and ran toward the small village that had grown up around the temple complex, and Diomedes and his men took off after them, bellowing war cries and brandishing their weapons. Achilles started to move in the same direction, but Patroclos stopped him.

"Let him go," Patrocles said. "There is nothing in that village but peasants. The real prize is in there," and he pointed to the main temple that stood fronting the plaza. Achilles smiled and nodded his assent.

All three temples on the plaza were similar, but the one Patroclos chose was the largest. There were temples throughout Greece, but nothing like the large, colonnaded structured that rose before them. Travelers had returned from the land of the Pharaohs with tales of huge triangular buildings and temples enclosed by tall marble columns and arches so tall that elephants could pass through without brushing their sides or their heads, but nobody believed that such buildings really existed.

Achilles, Patroclos, and their followers stood in awe in front of the magnificent structure, but it was only after Achilles had led his men up the steps from the plaza to the portico, that the men, staring directly up at the columns that loomed over them, could fully appreciate the immense scale of the building. The columns were so thick that two men could not wrap their arms around them, and so tall that no one could conceive how the massive marble pieces were raised to such a height.

"It must have been built by giants," Achilles said.

"Or by the gods themselves," Patroclos added.

When they tired of looking up, they looked straight ahead. Inside was another set of steps, and on top of them, another, smaller, temple, columned like the larger temple. They climbed the steps. And when they reached the top were able to see inside where a larger-than-life statue of Apollo stood on a raised platform holding a bow in his right hand and a lyre in his left; a quiver of arrows rested on his back. His head was raised, his eyes staring at the night sky. The moonlight, streaming in from the open roof, glinted off the gilded statue.

"Magnificent," murmured Patrocles in awe of the artistry.

"Gold," said Achilles.

"What?"

"The arrows are gold, and the lyre too. You were right Patroclos, this is far better than raiding a bunch of peasants' huts."

"You would strip the statue of its gold?"

"I am not like you or your friend Sinon. I am no lover of art, and I have no fear of the gods."

"I have no fear of them also, but it's not wise to provoke them."

"Maybe you should have stayed at home with Sinon and played with the horse he is making for you. Maybe you are getting too old for manly pursuits."

Patroclos was barely 18 when Achilles, in his early 20's and already a great hero, singled him out from a group of athletes exercising in the gymnasium. He loved Achilles from that day, and in spite of the rumors that constantly circulated around him as he grew into a handsome, sophisticated young man desired by both men and women, he had remained faithful to Achilles to this day, so he bristled at Achilles' comment.

"if by manly pursuits," he responded testily, "you mean butchering helpless peasants, raping women, and desecrating temples, then you are right. I have always been too old for that, and I thought you too noble."

Achilles looked at Patroclos with surprise. He was not used to being scolded, but he kept his composure. "We are not here to argue, Patroclos," he said. "There is work to do, whether it is to your taste or not."

He directed two of his men to begin stripping the gold from the statue and turned his attention to a structure that stood behind the statue. Like the other parts of the temple, this structure was colonnaded, but the columns were smaller, and the space between them had been closed over and an arched roof added.

"What do you make of this?" Achilles asked.

"Looks like a storeroom, Patroclos answered.

He had no trouble opening the door, which, to his surprise, had been bolted from the inside. He drew his sword and entered the dark room. "Light!" he bellowed, and one of his soldiers appeared with an oil lamp that been on a stand next to the statue of Apollo.

Patrocles was right. It was a storeroom. The walls were lined with shelves, all glistening with small golden objects, mostly images of the god, Apollo, all offerings from the people of Troy.

"Take them," Achilles said, and several of his men stripped off their shirts, made them into sacks, and began filling them with the gold offerings.

The small room was stuffy, so Patroclos walked outside to get some fresh air and to make sure that no Trojan troops were on their way, for by now Diomedes' men were hard at work killing, raping and ransacking the village, and someone had, no doubt, either sounded an alarm or escaped to alert the Trojans.

As he walked alongside the storeroom, he noticed that the walls extended beyond the length of the storeroom. He called Achilles.

"Look," he said, "there must be another room."

Achilles realized immediately that Patroclos was right and concluded that the room must contain even more treasure than the small storeroom. He began banging on the walls, looking for a weak spot or a secret door. He found the latter.

The door sprang open. "Light!" Achilles called, and once again, a soldier appeared holding a lamp aloft. The room was much larger than the storeroom, and the light from the lamp barely penetrated the darkness. Achilles looked around in a high state of excitement. He was sweating, both from the closeness of the air in the room and from excitement at the thought of the riches that he would soon find.

The room was richly furnished, but not with golden statues or urns, as he had hoped to find. There were large braziers for light, and chairs, tables, divans, and other household furnishings, all of excellent quality.

"What are we looking at here?" Achilles asked Patroclos.

"I am not sure," Patroclos answered. Then he could not help adding, "Perhaps they save these quarters for Apollo when he comes down to visit."

"What has gotten into you today?" Achilles growled.

"Sssh!" Patroclos said. "I hear something."

Both men grew silent and listened intently.

"There!" Patroclos whispered. "Did you hear it? It sounded like a child whimpering. It's coming from the back of the room."

"LIGHT!" Achilles roared. A second soldier appeared with another lamp, and all four men advanced into the darkness. They came to a black curtain that had been drawn across the entire width of the room, completely blocking the light from penetrating any further. Achilles and Patroclos readied their swords, pulled the curtain aside, and stared in disbelief at what stood before them.

One of the soldiers holding an oil lamp dropped to his knees and whispered, "goddess." The other stood mute with his eyes as large as saucers.

Standing before them was a beautiful woman in a diaphanous gown studded with tiny diamonds that sparkled in the flickering light of the oil lamps, revealing her long shapely legs, narrow hips and full breasts. Her long black hair cascaded down over her shoulders to her hips in a series of waves and curls. Her eyes, under long black lashes, shone as black as her hair, and her head was crowned with a tiara studded with precious gems. She neither moved nor spoke.

Achilles whispered to Patroclos, "Is she real? Or is this more artistry?"

"She is real. Did I not tell you that the real prize was in here?"

"She is most certainly a great prize. I was wise to heed your advice."

"And I to give it."

"Who are you?" Achilles demanded, "and why are you here?"

"Who are *you*," the woman responded, "and why are *you* here?"

"I am Achilles, Lord of the Myrmidons, son of the Nereid Thetis, and I am here to take you home as a prize to my father, Peleus, King of Pythia."

"I am Pythia, high priestess of Apollo, and I am no man's prize."

"And who is that hiding behind you?" Patroclos asked.

"My acolyte, Phemenoe," She responded. "Step forward girl. These men will not harm you."

Phemenoe stepped out from behind Pythia, and it was like a bright sun rising out of a black night. Her appearance drew gasps from the men who could not tell whether she stepped out from behind Pythia or grew out from her. It was as if she were Pythia's other self.

She was shorter than Pythia, just a child, at that androgynous age when children are neither all male nor all female. Her skin was pale and smooth, as yet untouched by life. Her golden hair was cut short. She wore a simple white silk shift that clung to her small body and revealed the beginnings of breasts. Her blue eyes glowed in the half-light.

"She will not speak," Pythia said. "She communes only with Apollo and with me."

She did not have to speak. Words were unnecessary. Her aura filled the room and softened the hearts of the men. Where Pythia was sensuous, alluring, and dangerous, she was innocence, purity, and warmth. She might as well have been the god of love, Eros, so completely were they entranced by her.

It was Patroclos who broke the spell. "We must go," he said. "I smell smoke. Those idiots must have set fire to the village. It's sure to be seen in Troy. If we don't hurry, we'll have the entire Trojan army to deal with."

Achilles turned to the two men holding the lamps. "Bind these two and take them to the ship. Treat them well. If any harm comes to them, you will pay with your lives."

He and Patroclos left to gather the rest of their men, and together they all headed quickly back to the boat.

"Do we wait for Diomedes?" Patroclos asked, nervously eyeing the red glow in the sky.

Achilles studied the sky. "It will be dark yet a while," he said. Then he turned to the ship's captain and asked about the tide and was told that the tide would hold for a little while longer. Achilles directed him to have the boat ready to move on a moment's notice, and then he told Patroclos to see about their 'trophies.'

The gold was stacked neatly in one corner of the bow, and the two women were seated on the floor next to it.

Patroclos grabbed the closest man to him and nearly strangled him while telling him, red-necked and full of rage, to gather something for the women to sit on and wrap themselves in to protect them from the chill on the water.

He was about to apologize to the women for their ill-treatment when there was an uproar and the boat filled with the sound of laughing men and clanging armor as Diomedes and his men jumped aboard.

"Away!" shouted Achilles, and the boatsmen poled the boat away from the shore into the middle of the stream where the quick current grabbed it and headed it seaward even before the oarsman could begin pulling.

Patroclos grabbed five men and stationed them in front of the women and the gold. "No one," he said, "gets past you except Achilles and me. If anyone tries, kill him. If you fail to do so, I will kill you—slowly. Do you understand?"

The men nodded that they understood and probably wondered what they had done to deserve such duty. Everyone else was in high spirits while they sat somber guard duty under Patroclos' steady glare.

Diomedes was happy. He and his men had looted the town, raped the women, and killed a few Trojans. It was, for them, a perfect night's work.

* * * *

Cassandra's Dream

Helen found her. She was laying on the floor by the door to her apartments. Her nails were torn and her knuckles bloodied. Blood was spattered on her face and her gown. Helen dropped to the floor and cradled her in her arms. She called the maids and sent for Paris.

She had run to Cassandra as soon as she heard about the raid on the temple. When she arrived, she found the door locked from the outside, but there was no guard in attendance. It was a simple slide bolt, so she opened it herself and found Cassandra. The maids, except for one elderly woman, were useless. The younger maids were afraid of Cassandra and reluctant to come too close to her, so Helen and the old woman had to tend to her until Paris arrived.

"We have to get her on to the bed," Helen said. "Do you think you can manage?"

The maid nodded her assent, and Helen took Cassandra under her arms and lifted her halfway up. The old lady, who was much stronger than she looked, locked her arms under Cassandra's knees, and together, they carried her easily to the bed.

The maid left immediately and quickly returned with a pan of water and some linens. Helen applied a cool compress to

Cassandra's forehead while the old woman removed Cassandra's soiled garments and began washing her. Cassandra remained unconscious and restless, tossing back and forth in the bed and muttering.

"What is she saying?" Helen wondered aloud.

"She is talking with the god," the old woman said, speaking for the first time and scaring Helen half to death.

"Do you understand any of it?"

"I am old," the woman said, "but not immortal. I understand no more than you."

Helen and the old woman continued to clean and calm Cassandra, and by the time Paris arrived, she was quietly sleeping.

"Thank the gods you are here," Helen said when Paris entered the room.

Paris walked to Cassandra's bedside and asked, "How long has she been unconscious?"

"I don't know," Helen answered. "She was like this when I came in."

"She had fallen just before you entered," the old lady said.

"She was alone!"

"Not alone," the woman said. "Apollo was with her."

"The maids wouldn't come when I summoned them— except for this one here. She has been very helpful."

Helen had seldom seen Paris angry, but now he turned purple with rage. "How dare they!" he demanded. "They will pay for this." He was about to say more but stopped when he saw Cassandra's hands. "What is this?" he asked.

"I found her on the floor by the door. I think she was trying to get out."

Paris sent the old lady to find the Captain of the Guard, then he returned to Cassandra's bedside.

"Will she live?" Helen asked.

"She will," Paris answered.

"How can you be sure?"

"She is my twin. If she were dying, I would know it. Besides, I am sure she has much to tell us, and Cassandra would never die and leave a tale untold."

When the Captain of the Guard arrived, Paris drew him aside and asked, "Why was my sister left unattended?"

"When the alarm went out that the Greeks had attacked the temple, they went to their combat stations."

"And no one was left here to protect or serve my sister?"

The captain looked uncomfortable. He hesitated before speaking. "One man should have remained," He said.

"I want that man found and dealt with. And I want the two maids who refused to help dealt with also. I believe you will find them cowering in their quarters."

"Dealt with how? Sir."

"Severely."

"And the maids too?"

"The maids too."

"What was that about?" Helen asked when Paris returned to the bedside.

"I told him I wanted the guards and the maids replaced. They are not suitable."

"I agree. I cannot understand how they could have left her unattended and in pain."

"Pythia!" Cassandra sat up, her eyes wide with fear, "Pythia!" she said again. Sweat poured down her face, and her hands trembled. She looked at Paris but did not see him.

"Cassandra," Helen soothed. "It's all right. You're going to be all right."

But Cassandra didn't respond. She looked directly at Helen but didn't see her.

"What is wrong with her," Helen asked.

"Nothing," Paris answered. "The god is with her. She is looking at something we cannot see. She will come back to us in time. Sit with her and don't worry. She will recover. I must return to my post."

* * *

Paris returned to the ramparts to find everything quiet. He could not see any activity in the Greek camp. Hector approached him and asked where he had gone. "To Cassandra," he replied.

"Is she unwell?" Hector asked.

"She will recover." He needed to say no more. Hector understood.

Hector had not sent any troops to the temple, having concluded that it was a feint, designed to draw troops away from the city. He felt that the damage there had been done, and nothing he could do would help. He knew that the Greeks would leave only the dead behind, and they would wait until the dawn without complaint. But the fact that the Greeks did not attack confused him.

He called the Keeper of the Gate and told him to summon Sinon. "Maybe he can tell us what is going on," he said.

* * *

Paris returned to Cassandra's room to find her sitting up and alert.

"Look," Helen said happily, "Your sister has returned to us."

"I never doubted she would. When we were children, we promised each other that since we came into this world together, we would leave it together. And, as I am alive, so must she be."

"Do not tease, brother. We are too close to death for jokes."

Paris became serious at once. "What have you seen sister?"

"I have seen death brother."

"Ours?"

"No, many people on both sides..."

"That is the nature of war."

"...but one in particular."

"Who?"

"Achilles."

* * * *

Pythia and Phemenoe

As soon as Achilles returned from the raid, he distributed the booty among his men, preserving only Pythia and the gold from Apollo's statue for himself. He then offered Patroclos first choice of all that remained. Patroclos chose Phemenoe, and nothing more.

"Don't you want any of the gold?" Achilles asked.

"Phemenoe is more precious and more rare than gold."

Achilles was baffled. "I know she looks like a boy, but she is female."

"I know the difference between males and females."

Still puzzled, Achilles asked, "Then have you changed your taste in your old age?"

"I am neither old, nor different than what I always was. It is not a matter of taste, nor as you think, a matter of sex."

"What is it, then?"

"Beauty, but I don't really expect you to understand that. Even though you are one of the most beautiful men on Earth, you neither understand nor appreciate beauty in others."

"Nor do I understand you, Patroclos. You excel in the gymnasium and are courageous in battle, yet you fawn over pretty trinkets like a schoolgirl. I will never understand that about you."

"Good. There should always be a little mystery between us."

"What will you do with her?"

"Not what you would do, and that is one of the reasons I want her."

"If you do not intend to use her, what *will* you do with her?"

"Protect her. And what will you do with Pythia?"

"Enjoy her."

"And what if she refuses to be enjoyed?"

"You know the answer to that as well as I do."

"And now you know why I must protect Phemenoe."

* * *

Patrocles took Phemenoe to his tent and left her in the care of Sinon who was not happy when he learned that she was an acolyte in the Temple of Apollo.

"It was the priests from that temple who stoned my mother to death," he said.

"Priests, not priestesses," Patroclos responded. "And certainly not this young girl."

Sinon agreed that Patroclos was right and promised to look after Phemenoe, but just to make sure she would be safe, Patroclos posted two guards outside his tent and gave strict orders that no one except he and Sinon were to enter.

"Not even the Great king himself?" asked one of the guards.

"Especially not him," Patrocles answered.

124

Satisfied that Phemenoe was safe for the time being, he returned to Achilles' tent in time to find him roughly tossing Pythia into bed.

"Bad timing?"

"Bah!" Achilles grunted. "The woman is as cold and hard as one of those marble statues you are so fond of. I should have given her to you. You could have put her on a pedestal and admired her. Zeus knows, she is good for little else."

"It's not too late. But I will not give you Phemenoe in exchange."

"What will you give me? Name it, and she is yours."

"Advice."

"Advice! I have no need of advice—especially from you. How do you dare to offer advice to *me*?"

"I dare because I love you. Will you hear me?"

Patroclos' words softened Achilles' anger. He sank into a seat, poured a cup of wine, and said, "Speak."

"I must speak to Pythia."

"Why?"

"because Phemenoe spoke to me, but in a language I do not understand..."

"*She spoke to you!*" Pythia gasped.

"Yes," Patroclos replied, "but I did not understand her. I thought you might."

"Tell me what she said."

Patroclos repeated the words Phemenoe spoke to him.

Pythia listened intently, and then turned her black eyes on Achilles. Had he been a lesser man, he would have shuddered under her steady gaze. He didn't falter, but he did slam his cup down on the table and shout, "WELL, ARE YOU GOING TO SPEAK, OR MUST I GUESS?"

"You have angered Apollo," she said. "He bids me remind you that you chose a short, glorious life."

"I know this! Is this the best your god can do?"

"You are approaching your 30th year."

Pythia stated this without emotion, and Achilles received it without emotion, but Patroclos noticed a slight shift in his body from one side to the other as if he had just absorbed a punch. *It is one thing to talk about the glory of dying young,* Patroclos thought, *it is quite another to face up to the reality of it.*

Achilles turned to Patroclus. "You wanted to give me some advice," he said blandly.

"Let's go home, Achilles. There is no glory here, only an inglorious death from starvation and disease. You have your victory. You plundered the Temple of Apollo and captured the High Priestess. You said yourself that she is like a statue, suited only to be admired—so let her be admired. Bring her home and show her to the people. There is nothing more here to be accomplished."

"I cannot abandon the others, not while there is still a chance to take Troy. It would be cowardly."

"The others have already threatened to leave unless Menelaus orders an assault on the citadel, and he won't do that. If you go, the others will follow."

Achilles sat back in his chair and poured another cup of wine. 'I don't like it, but will think on it," he said.

* * * *

The Crafty Odysseus

The Greek army was, for the most part, a rapidly thrown together patchwork of rowdy young men and roughnecks in search of adventure. The only exceptions to this were the Spartans and the Ithakans, and to some extent the Myrmidons, who obeyed Achilles. Consequently, when word of Achilles and Diomedes' successful raid on the temple became known among the Greeks, many of the men, tired of the tedium of camp living, decided to try their luck in the hopes that not all the booty or women had been taken.

The night following Achilles' return, about 100 Mycenaeans commandeered a pair of barges and had them towed to the mouth of the Scamander. They rowed up river until they came within walking distance of the temple. They disembarked, joking and laughing as they walked to the temple, expecting to find an abandoned village and maybe, if they were lucky, some sport. They did not expect to find a contingent of Trojan cavalry.

The disorganized, leaderless Greeks fell quickly under the swords of the Trojans, and the few who were able to escape to the barges were harassed all the way back to the delta by archers hiding in the tall grass along the riverbank. They were too few to pole the boats over the sandbar, so they jumped into the shallow water and tried to swim to the safety of the trireme waiting offshore. In the end only two men made it safely home.

* * *

That was a month ago, and Odysseus was still furious every time he thought about it. He didn't care about the men who were lost. He did care about the fresh water and food supplies that had been lost.

The day after Achilles' raid, Hector posted archers along the river and ordered his cavalry to patrol the entire temple area, which was why the Mycenaeans were greeted so rudely when they arrived, and why Odysseus had to suspend all future supply trips.

Diomedes had satisfied his need for blood, and Achilles his need for prizes, but their actions cost the Greeks their access to fresh food and water. The supplies that Odysseus brought back lasted only two weeks, so for the last two weeks, the Greeks had been reduced to eating the last of the grain they had brought with them and drinking undiluted wine, which was also in short supply. The men were bored, angry, and growing rebellious.

Odysseus realized that something had to be done before the men grew so angry that they mutinied. He also realized that Achilles was the key to holding the men together. He had a plan, but it would require Achilles' endorsement to succeed, so, as soon as the plan was set in his mind, he visited the Myrmidon camp where he found Achilles and Patroclus lounging over a late breakfast.

"Sleep well?" he said in greeting.

"We have little else to do here," said Patroclos.

"I am glad to find you so well rested, for *I* have use of your services."

"If you come from the King, you will be disappointed." Achilles said.

"Agamemnon does not know that I am here."

"Speak then. I will listen."

"Are your Myrmidons tired of building a wall?"

"Very."

"And would they enjoy and outing?"

"What kind of outing?" Patroclos asked.

"One in which they could exercise their swords, and Achilles could enter the field with honor."

"Do not speak in riddles," Achilles said. "Out with it. What do you propose?"

"It is very simple. You know we need supplies. And you also know our ships cannot break the Trojan blockade without armed escort..."

"And to do that," Patroclos interjected, "would severely weaken our defenses and invite an attack."

"Exactly. I propose that you take your Myrmidons and leave."

"WHAT?"

"Take your men and your ships and sail out of the harbor. The Trojan fleet wouldn't dare attack, but Hector might. After Agamemnon's disgraceful retreat, they fear only the great Achilles..."

"And," Patroclos noted, "if they see Achilles leave, they will attack."

"I cannot agree to this. I will be at sea when they attack. It would be cowardly."

Patroclos laughed. "He means to bring you back, Achilles! To save the day for the Greeks. Isn't that so Odysseus?"

"Yes. You will escort the cargo ships past the blockade, and then turn around and come back in time to save us from Hector."

"Can you hold the Trojans long enough?"

"We can hold them, but your men will have to row hard, or we will all be lost."

"What do you think of this Patroclos? Do you still advise going home?"

"Not if there is a chance for glory."

"We will be there, Odysseus, even if I have to carry the ships on my back."

"Good. Then if you are agreed, I will consult with Diomedes and Ajax."

"Not with Agamemnon," Achilles said. "I insist. He must know nothing."

"You have my word. I will speak neither with him nor his brother."

"I am agreed."

* * *

Odysseus did not speak with the King or his brother, but as soon as he left Achilleas, he went to see Nestor. He approached the old man cautiously, unsure of whether he could be trusted or not.

"Something must be done," he said. "Storming the walls isn't going to work."

"I agree," Nestor replied. "but we cannot sit and wait to starve to death. I tried to convince them that Troy was too hard a nut to crack, but the war hawks would not listen. In their hubris and arrogance, they thought they could come here and blow the walls down, or perhaps the Trojans would run away in fear of the mighty Achilles. They have learned a bitter lesson."

"What do they plan now?"

"Nothing. They are in complete confusion. They argue and blame each other for this failure. And no one dares to point out that the mighty Achilles, whose voice was loudest in favor of this war, has decided to sit in his tent and sulk, rather than fight."

"I might have a solution, but it would require delicacy."

Nestor laughed. "Of course you have a solution. Are you not the cunning Odysseus, the favorite of Athena, the wisest of the gods? I must apologize to you Odysseus. Calchas insisted on your presence here, but it was I who engineered it. It pained me to take you away from your wife and child, but the fate of the Greek nation depends on you and your brain, not on the strength of Ajax, not the ferocity of Diomedes, or even the skill of Achilles. All of that is nothing against the strength of Troy. We will defeat Troy through wisdom and trickery, and who better than Odysseus of Ithaka to lead us?"

"And who better than Nestor of Pylos to aid me? Do I have your help?"

"Let me hear your plan, and I will tell you."

Odysseus described his plan to draw Hector into an attack on the barricade.

"And Achilles has agreed to this?"

"Yes, on the condition that Agamemnon knows nothing of it."

"That is easily done. Agamemnon knows little of anything these days. He grows madder by the minute."

"What of Menelaus?"

"He can be trusted."

"And Diomedes and Ajax?"

"Promise them blood and they will be your friends."

"Good. We are set then. You will speak with Menelaus, and I with the others. Tomorrow, at the rising of the sun, Achilles and his Myrmidons will sail away, and with a little luck, Hector will take the bait."

"Oh, he will take the bait, for I have already set the trap."

"How? How have you done this?"

"I have a spy, a lover of Patroclos who hates the Trojans. I sent him to Hector with an exaggerated tale of dissension in our ranks. I had thought only to give him false information, but as it turns out, things are coming together nicely. I see the hand of your patron, Athena, in this."

"If you are right, we cannot fail."

* * * *

The Death of Heroes

Hector climbed hurriedly to the top of the wall in response to an urgent summons from the Captain of the Watch. The sun had not yet risen, but a red glow outlined the horizon, making it just possible to see a large group of black dots crawling silently across the dark blue surface of the sea.

"Are they leaving?" The Captain asked.

"Perhaps," was all Hector would say.

He was joined on the ramparts by Aeneas, who looked over the scene unfolding in the Greek camp.

"What do you see?" Hector asked.

"Confusion. Panic."

"Is it real, or faked?"

"It seems real enough. Those are Achilles' ships leaving, and he has decamped. There is not a stick left standing in his encampment. And he has left a huge gap in the center of their line."

"Still," Hector mused, "it could be a ruse to draw us out."

"If it is a ruse, and we attack the weak point in the line, as they seem to be inviting us to do, the center will collapse and the Spartans and Ithakans will flank us and fold us inside. It's a classic tactic."

"Who is in the center?"

"It looks like the Mycenaeans are filling in. But Ajax is on one side and Diomedes on the other. I can't see either of those two falling back."

Hector laughed. "You have been of no help," he said. "You are our expert on military strategy, and all you have done is to confuse me further...*Captain!*"

"Yes sir."

"I believe you know Sinon?"

"Yes sir."

"Is he in the Greek camp now?"

"Yes sir. I let him through the gates last night."

"Can you get him back?"

"It is getting light. It will be hard, but the shadows are still long. I can try sir."

"Do more than try, Captain. I must speak to this man, and quickly."

Paris arrived on the ramparts, and seeing Hector pacing back and forth, decided to leave him alone and talk instead with Aeneas, who was intently following events on the beach.

"What's going on?" Paris asked.

"Achilles has apparently decided to go home," Aeneas answered dryly.

"That's great news!" Paris exclaimed.

"Perhaps." Aeneas answered.

"You smell a rat?"

"I do."

"And Hector?"

"Waiting for a report from his spy."

After what seemed to be an agonizingly long time, two
men appeared atop the ramparts, rapidly approaching Hector.
Paris recognized one of the men as the Captain of the Guard.
The other he did not know. Hector drew the man aside, while
Paris and Aeneas watched for any hint of what they might be
saying.

Hector dismissed the man, and as he and the Captain left,
turned to Paris and Aeneas.

"What did he say?" Paris asked as soon as Hector was
within speaking distance.

"He confirms that Achilles has left. He refuses to follow
the King any longer. Diomedes and Ajax were only convinced
to remain after Agamemnon agreed to put Menelaus in
charge of the army, but that wasn't good enough for Achilles.
The Greeks are disorganized and disheartened. He urges us to
strike now."

"And will we?"

"I'm not sure. What is your advice Aeneas?"

"We attack, but cautiously. We will attack in two waves.
Hector will lead the first, and I will lead the second. Paris you
are to organize the charioteers and cavalry and hold them in
reserve. I will withhold my forces until I see that Hector has
breached the barricade. At that point, I expect the Greek
flanks to fold in and try to encircle him. I will launch my
attack at that time.

"Paris, only leave these walls if it becomes absolutely
necessary. I do not want to have to commit the last of our
forces."

"I understand. Good luck to you both."

* * *

The Greek camp was a mass of confusion—or at least that is how Odysseus hoped it would appear to the Trojans watching from the wall. From time to time, he stopped barking orders long enough to look up at the Trojans who were looking down at him. He had no trouble locating Hector. He wondered if Hector could find him among the crowd of soldiers milling around him. Hector could not, but Aenaes, who was the better military man, had an eye for such things. He searched out all the Greek commanders and noted where each was and what he was doing.

He still had his doubts, but the opportunity could not be passed up. He nodded at Hector; the gates swung open, and the Trojans poured out shouting their war cry.

Odysseus waited until the Trojan army was half-way to the barricade and fully committed to the assault before signaling for the bonfire at the end of the beach to be lit. This was Achilles' signal to turn his ships around and return to join the battle.

Hector, leading the charge down the beach, could not see the signal, nor could Aenaes, who was forming up his troops inside the walls. Paris, however, saw it immediately from his perch on the ramparts. At first, he didn't pay a lot of attention to it because he was so intent on the battle that was unfolding before him. He followed his brother's every move, watching with pride and excitement as Hector, in his battle chariot, fearlessly lead his troops in a direct assault on the

Greeks' earthen barricade. Cretan bowmen waited until the Trojans were in close range and then released volley after volley of arrows, but Hector never faltered. He brought his chariot to the base of the barricade and jumped from it to the top of the defensive wall as arrows flew all around him and spears bounced off his shield. From his position on top of the barricade, he rallied his troops before vaulting off the wall into the middle of the Greek forces. It was only when Hector was no longer visible that Paris took note of the bonfire, which was now fully blazing and would be visible from miles away. Then it dawned on him and he looked to the sea— Achilles' ships were rowing hard toward the beach!

Neither Hector, who had breached the wall and was fully engaged in battle, nor Aeneas, who, as planned, was leading his troops down the beach in support, could see what Paris saw.

As soon as Hector breached the barricade, the center of the Greek line started to collapse. The Mycenaeans were routed, while Diomedes on one side and Ajax on the other began a slower, more orderly retreat.

Odysseus looked on with satisfaction. Hector was being sucked into the trap. His troops, intent on slaughtering the fleeing Mycenaeans, were being hemmed in. Odysseus ordered his troops to wheel to the right and close the trap on Hector. Menelaus issued a similar order to his Trojans.

However, the plan wasn't quite perfect. Aeneas was on his way to reinforce Hector. His troops would arrive just as Odysseus and Menelaus were attempting to swing their forces around and would require them to fight Aeneas on one side, and Hector on the other.

Odysseus saw this. He was not surprised. He expected a reserve force and was confident his Ithakans and Menelaus' Spartans could hold them until Achilles arrived. Victory or defeat would turn on the strength and skill of Achilles' oarsmen.

The beach was jammed with combatants packed together so closely that some of the men could not find enough room to swing their swords. Some stood nose-to-nose with their enemy and were unable to strike a blow. But, despite this, there was mayhem enough. The sand was stained red with blood. It ran in rivulets to the sea. So many were slaughtered that those who could still fight had to stand on the corpses of those who had fallen.

Diomedes and Ajax were covered in blood as they cut and hacked their way in a vain attempt to reach Hector, who, surrounded by his honor guard, had fought his way completely through the Greek forces until he reached the sea, where he ordered his men to set fire to the Greeks' ships.

The Greek and Trojan forces were gripped in violent hand-to hand combat. Order and discipline had dissolved into a wild melee. It was butchery on both sides, with neither seeming to have an advantage.

It was at this point that Achilles' ships reached the beach. As soon as the prow of his ship touched solid ground, Achilles issued a tremendous roar and jumped into the middle of the fray, followed closely behind by Patroclos.

From his station on the ramparts, Paris watched as the black-clad Myrmidons swarmed on to the beach like an army of ants devouring everything in their way. Down on the beach, the view was not as clear. The Myrmidons had stepped ashore into the middle of a chaotic mass of fighting men and burning ships. The air was filled with smoke, cinders, grunts, groans, and screams as men blindly fought one another in the semi-darkness.

Achilles loved it. Patroclos thought he had been dropped into Hades. Neither man could see anything other than what was right in front of them. They could barely make out the figure of Hector, surrounded by his honor guard, barking out orders to his captains. They tried to fight their way through the crush of humans that stood between them, but were hindered by the Mycenaeans, who had rejoined the battle when Achilles made his appearance. Hemmed in on all sides by friend and foe alike, they struck out indiscriminately in their attempt to reach Hector.

Hector was surrounded too, as Diomedes closed in on him from one side and Ajax Major from the other. The added pressure from Achilles and his Myrmidons was causing his honor guard to buckle, but despite the relentless onslaught, he managed to find Achilles in the crush of combatants. He carefully chose his heaviest spear, offered a prayer to Ares, and launched it at Achilles, who was fully engaged and did not see it coming. Patroclos, however, saw it, and realizing that Achilles was exposed and unprepared to defend himself, acted without hesitation. He placed himself between Achilles and the spear that was hurtling towards him.

Had he had one second more, his effort would have been successful, one short second spelled the difference between life and death. Had he had that one second more, he would have had time to position himself correctly to receive that spear properly. He would have been able to set his body squarely in front of the oncoming missile. It would have struck his shield dead center and shattered. But he did not have that one second more. He was still on the move when the spear hit his shield. It struck just above the mid-point, and had it been thrown by anybody other than Hector, it probably would have shattered or fallen harmlessly to the ground, but Hector was strong, enormously strong, and the spear he had chosen was of solid oak. It hit the top of Patroclos' shield with such force that the shield tipped backward and the spear, following the angle of the shield upward, entered Patroclos' throat under his chin guard and exited the back of his neck, severing his spinal cord. Patroclos fell dead at Achilles' feet.

Achilles roared in grief at the sight of his dead lover, and spying Hector, began a ferocious assault on the Trojan forces that stood between him and his enemy.

Paris had watched in horror as Achilles overwhelmed everything in their way. He could see what Hector could not—Achilles was pushing the Trojans back, slowly but surely collapsing their defenses, leaving Hector and his small honor guard isolated.

He decided. He descended from the walls, leapt on to his war chariot and ordered the cavalry into action. The great gates of the citadel swung open, and the Trojan cavalry poured onto the field.

Odysseus saw the cavalry leave the gates and immediately ordered his men to pull back and form a defensive wall. The Ithakan and Spartan forces were outside the barricade in the open and no match for cavalry and battle chariots. There was no time to get back to the protection of the barricade, so all they could do was regroup, shield-to-shield, as best they could. There was hardly a man who was not wounded. Those who couldn't stand would have to lay where they were and pray that their death would be quick. Illotos was among them. Lipos helped him to his feet and propped him up in line.

"DOWN! DOWN!" Kretin shouted.

Illotos dropped to the ground and curled up under his shield. He heard the thunder of hoofs and felt the earth shake. And then everything went black.

Paris wasted no time, neither with the Ithakans nor the Spartans, but went straight into the melee in an attempt to reach his brother. Ahead of him, he could see Aeneas ripping a hole in the Greek forces, trying to reach Hector who was surrounded on all sides by black helmets, killing all who came within his sword's reach. But a sword is useless against spears and arrows, and Paris knew that Hector was lost. He watched helplessly as the great hero slowly sagged under the weight of numerous wounds. An arrow struck the back of his leg, severing his hamstring. He fell to one knee. His sword fell from his hand.

Achilles loomed over him. Snarled some insult and raised his sword. Paris ordered his charioteer to stop and quiet the horses. The man knew what to do. The horses did too, and ignoring the noise and turmoil around them, stood perfectly still.

Paris chose his shaft carefully, nocked it with precision, and aimed carefully. He did not rush the shot. Hector was lost. He knew it. This arrow would not save him. Achilles was clad in his famous bronze armor. It covered him from head to toe. It took a strong man to carry that much weight into battle, and Achilles was a strong man. That armor, supposedly forged by the smithy god Hephaestus in his forge on Olympus, was protection against any mortal arrow. There was only one small spot left unprotected. His shot would have to be perfect. He uttered a prayer to Apollo and let fly. The arrow whizzed through the air, straight and true, through the eyehole in Achilles' helmet, piercing the eye and burying itself in his brain. Achilles' head snapped back, and then he pitched forward, falling dead in front of Hector who only lived long enough to witness his brother's victory.

* * * *

A Time for Weeping

Darkness brought an end to the killing, but not the suffering. The sky was clear and lit by billions of stars. A crescent moon shone brightly, and below it, Ares' planet, a red blot on an otherwise brilliant sky, looked longingly at Aphrodite, the brightest star in the galaxy. It was a beautiful night, or at least it might have been if it weren't pierced by the keening and wailing of the women inside the walls of Troy and the groans and calls for help from the wounded left behind on the battlefield. The men on duty on the ramparts had to stuff their ears with wax or go mad. They were not alone. The Greeks, in their tents and ships, also heard the cries and beat their chests and wept.

The Ithakans and the Spartans had suffered terrible losses, first from Aenaes' assault, and then from Paris' cavalry charge. The cheering and bravado of the prior two nights was gone. Odysseus and Kretin moved among the men, consoling them on their losses and praising them for their courage. Odysseus stopped when he came to the litter where Illotos lay wounded. He looked at Lipos, cut and bruised, soaked in his own blood, but still standing.

"He will live," Lipos said.

"Only because you were there to protect him. Thank you."

Lipos didn't answer, and Odysseus passed on to the man on the next litter. Almost every Ithakan had sustained some sort of injury, Even Kretin was walking around with his arm heavily bandaged.

"Do we count today as a victory?" Kretin asked.

"Some might. I do not. We could not survive another such victory."

"How is it with the others?"

"No better. Achilles and Patroclos are dead. Ajax is in his tent mortally wounded. The Myrmidons are done. They want to take Achilles home. They only came at his urging, and now they have no reason to stay. The Spartans took as many casualties as we did. They will fight if asked, but I don't think Menelaus will ask."

"Diomedes and the others?"

"Diomedes wants to stay and fight."

"He will be overruled in council?"

"He will."

"Then it is over."

"If the Trojans do not see our weakness and attack."

"They will not attack. They suffered as badly as we, maybe worse. We lost Achilles, a hero and a great warrior, but not our leader, not our heart and soul. They lost Hector. That is a much greater loss than Achilles. Do you hear the wailing coming from the behind those walls? That is not the sound of a victorious army eager for the next day's battle."

Kretin's assessment was right. The situation in Troy was no better than that of the Greek camp. Yesterday's cheers had turned to today's tears. There were no women in the Greek camp to wail for their men. That would come later when the ships returned without the men who filled their hulls when they left. But there were many women in Troy, and they wept bitterly and wailed for the loss of their husbands and sons. The weeping and wailing were not limited to commoners. The losses on both sides had been horrific and Death knew no social boundaries; it honored no titles. The rich as well as the poor; the noble as well as the peasant, all had been swept up in the carnage. No stratum of society had been spared.

Inside the palace, Queen Hecuba wept for her son and held tightly to Hector's wife, Andromeda, who wrapped her arms around Hector's infant son, Astyanax, and sobbed bitterly.

Helen wept too and clung tightly to Paris.

"What is to become of us now that he is gone?" she asked between tears.

"What is to become of Troy, now that he is gone?" Paris responded. "He was our rock. While he lived, we felt nothing could harm us. But now?"

"We must tell Cassandra."

"She knows without our telling."

"We should still speak with her. She needs us. She has no other."

Paris and Helen left their private quarters and made their way to that part of the palace where Cassandra was confined. The hallways were nearly deserted, but the sounds of sorrow coming from behind closed doors filled the palace and echoed through the near-empty corridors. Occasionally, they passed small groups of people, weeping and consoling each other. They turned their eyes away as Helen and Paris passed, whether out of compassion or contempt, the couple did not know.

There was more than sorrow in the halls; there was fear. It was palpable. Hector's death had taken everybody by surprise. Nobody had believed it could happen. But it had, and it left an emptiness that had been filled with dread, a feeling that something terrible was about to happen, something so horrible that it could not be expressed in words. It seeped into the walls and was inhaled with every breath. Helen and Paris were shaking by the time they reached Cassandra's apartment. They found her in the little, walled courtyard outside her bedroom, sitting quietly, weeping.

They exchanged concerned glances as they cautiously approached her.

"Sister?" Paris said softy.

Cassandra turned at the sound. She managed a small smile when she saw her brother and sister-in-law.

"Are you alright?" Paris asked.

"Yes, brother," she answered. "I am fine. But how are you?"

"Worried about you. You know about Hector?"

"I know. I was there when it happened. I saw his death."

Helen and Paris both exclaimed, "What!" at the same time.

"How can this be?" Paris asked.

"Apollo granted me a vision. Since I am not allowed to leave this palace, I cannot any longer perform my priestly functions at the temple, so I had a small altar erected here, and I was sacrificing to Apollo when I fell into a swoon. It was not a 'falling down.' I did not roll around and scream and bite my tongue as I have done in the past. This time, I fell into a deep sleep. Apollo came to me and took me by my hand. I know it was him. I tried to look at him, but the light that surrounded him was so bright that I had to turn my eyes away. And yet, I knew it was him. He lifted me out of myself. I thought I had died because I could look down and see myself on the floor, surrounded by anxious, fretting maids. The god granted me a vision—do not scoff brother. You, above all others, know I speak the truth."

"What did you see?" Helen said. "Please tell us."

"Scenes of such slaughter that my mind cannot comprehend it, nor my voice tell it. I saw Ares, all bloody, laughing, and I saw our noble Hector surrounded by a horde of black-clad soldiers, slaying them left and right so fast that the bodies piled up around him like a barrier. I saw spears and arrows coming at him from all sides, for they feared to approach within his sword's reach. He stood and dared them to approach, but none did."

"Did you see him fall?" Paris asked.

"He never fell. He dropped to one knee, overcome by wounds from scores of spears and arrows. Only then did the mighty Achilles dare to approach. He stood before Hector and raised his massive two-handed sword above his head. But before he could strike, I saw you, Paris. I saw you nock your arrow. I saw you aim, and I heard your prayer to Apollo. The god heard it too, and I watched as he guided your shaft straight and true. Hector saw too. I am sure of it, because as Achilles fell before him, I heard him speak your name."

Paris, Helen, and Cassandra held tightly to each other and wept.

"What is to become of us?" Helen asked when she was able to speak.

"You do not wish to know," Cassandra said.

"Has the god revealed our futures to you?"

"Mine yes, and Paris' too. Not yours. I will not speak of it, but I have already told you that I have seen Troy aflame."

"That will not be," Paris said. "Not all your visions are true, and in this case, I cannot credit your story. Our walls are still strong enough to repel an attack, even without Hector, and Aeneas has sent for reinforcements from the frontier. We can replenish out troops. The Greeks cannot. Their losses were as great as ours. They do not have the numbers to take us on again. They rolled the dice and lost. They will go home. They have no choice."

"I pray that you are right, and I am wrong."

* * * *

Penelope

Odysseus' property manager, Philoctius, stood before Penelope, nervously shifting his weight from one foot to the other while he waited for her to speak. He had no clear idea of what she would say—whether she would shout in anger or cry in despair, for the news that he had brought her was not good—no, it was worse than not good; it was downright bad, and he had every reason to expect a bad response.

Agamemnon had demanded that Odysseus provide ten ships, each with 100 men. In order to meet this demand, Odysseus had to heavily mortgage his lands. The loan was for one year, with half the payment in monthly food and livestock from his estates, and the balance at the end of the year. The bankers' representatives came once a month to collect the payment.

Philoctius had the burden of informing Penelope that, for the second month in a row, the estates had not produced enough to meet the payments. He explained that this was primarily due to his inability to hire enough laborers to work the fields and shepherd the flocks. Odysseus had taken most of the able-bodied young men with him, and those that remained were older men with families.

"They need to get paid," he explained. "They love Odysseus, and sympathize with your plight, but they cannot feed their families on promises. They must be paid, and we have no coin to pay them with. It all went to outfitting the ships."

"Where are these men working?' she asked sharply, "And who has coin to pay them?"

"Polybus. He has made a fortune on this war."

Penelope took this in without comment. She didn't ask Philoctius for more information, nor did she dismiss him. She left him standing and waiting, nervously anticipating some sort of fury or tantrum.

To his great relief and surprise, Penelope reacted neither with anger nor with tears.

"I thought," she said calmly, "That the bankers had agreed to a year."

"Yes, they had, but the contract states that if we default three months in a row, they can call in the loan, and that is what they plan to do."

"But we have only defaulted for two months."

"The third is inevitable. They know it and next month, they will come prepared to take over the property."

"What will they do with it?"

"Sell it."

"To Polybus."

"Most likely."

"Can this be prevented?"

"Not by any means within my control."

"If not yours, then whose?" she asked.

"Possibly yours, my Lady."

"How?"

"Polybus wants you more than he wants the property."

Penelope fell into another one of her silences. It was a long time before she spoke.

"Send word to Polybus. Tell him I would like to speak with him in two days' time. If he accepts, then go to Eumaeus and tell him to select a fine young lamb for slaughter. Now go, and on your way out tell the household staff to assemble. This place looks like a pig sty."

* * *

Eurycleia was worried. Demia was in her ninth month and had been bedridden for the last two. She was feverish, and at times hysterical, but she was quiet today.

She had seen this before. She had been delivering babies for more than fifty years, having learned at her mother's side, watching her as she went from hut to hut, administering her herbal remedies while also serving as midwife to half of Ithaka.

She had delivered Odysseus, *Now there was a difficult delivery!* she thought. *Even as a babe, he was broad-shouldered. How his poor mother suffered!*

She looked down at Demia. The girl murmured "Illotos," and stirred slightly.

"Rest my dear," the old nurse whispered, "you will need your strength."

Eumaeus entered the room, looked at Demia, and turned to Eurycleia.

"Will she live?" he asked.

"She will live!" the old woman scolded, "and the child as well. Do you think I am as old and useless as you?"

Eumaeus laughed. "You did not always think me so old and useless. I remember..."

"You barely remember what day it is. Why are you here? Surely it is not to torture me with your memories?"

"The Mistress wishes to know how Demia is progressing."

"Tell her all is well. It won't be long now."

"Will it be a boy or a girl?"

"How do I know?"

"They say in the village that you are a witch, just like your mother, and you know these things."

"They say a lot of foolish things in the village, and only a fool listens to them."

Eumaeus laughed again. "Your tongue is as sharp as your wit," he said, "and neither has dulled with time."

"Enough of your nonsense. Go away. Can't you see that I am busy here."

"I see more than you think I see. I see that you are worried—but do not fear. I will tell Penelope that all is well. But if there is anything I can do..."

"Fetch water and bring plenty of clean linens. We will have need of both soon. Send for the maids, and when you have done that, leave me. This is no place for a useless man."

* * *

Polybus had eagerly accepted Penelope's invitation, and showed up at the appointed time, clean, dressed in his finest clothes and accompanied by his son, Eurymachus, and two armed bodyguards. They passed through the gate unchallenged but were stopped by Nexios as they crossed the courtyard.

"You and your son may enter, but those two must go," he said.

Nexios was dressed in his full military apparel, and bore a sword, knife, spear and shield. He looked entirely capable of handling the two untrained thugs who accompanied Polybus.

"We are unarmed," Polybus replied. "and without these men, we will be at your mercy."

"You have been invited to dine with the Queen," Nexios responded. "You are guests in the house of King Odysseus. No harm will come to you here."

"We have not always been welcome in this house. How can we be sure we will be safe?"

"You have the word of Queen Penelope and the protection of Zeus. You need no more than that."

When Polybus hesitated, Nexios added, "Stay or go as you wish. The lamb will be eaten with or without you."

At the mention of the word 'lamb,' Polybus lifted his nose to the air and caught the pungent aroma of meat turning on a spit. Polybus was a simple man; he loved, in this order, money, power, and food. He desired Penelope, but he thought of her in terms of a delicacy, like wild mushrooms, to be tasted and enjoyed. He would be hard pressed to choose between her and a tender, sweet, roasted baby lamb. He would probably choose Penelope, because, in addition to being a treat to his senses, she brought along with her land, which was money, and prestige, which was power.

And so, at last, he dismissed his retainers and surrendered himself to his appetites.

Nexios stepped aside and let him and his son enter. They stepped into an entrance hall where they were met by a servant who escorted them to a large, open room with a great fireplace at one end. The room was empty except for Philoctius and Odysseus' father, Laertes. Both men rose when they entered.

Philoctius made a small bow. Laertes said, "Polybus, Eurymachus," and nodded his head.

Polybus and Eurymachus nodded in return, mumbled something unrecognizable that passed for a greeting, and looked around nervously.

"Penelope..." Polybus began, but was interrupted by Laertes who said, "...Will be here shortly. Please sit," and he indicated two chairs arranged opposite his and Philoctius'. The two guests sat. One servant entered and poured wine while another put a large tray of fruits and cheeses on the table in front of them.

Polybus and Eurymachus eyed them warily. Laertes took a sip of his wine, leaned over and scooped up a handful of fruit and nuts.

"Eat," he chuckled. "It's not poison. Be assured, if the Queen wanted you dead, she has friends enough to do the job. There would be no need for duplicity."

It was an empty threat. Penelope had friends, but not enough to take on Polybus and his gang of henchmen. However, in addition to being greedy and licentious, Polybus was also paranoid, especially when it came to Odysseus, who he feared more than anything or anyone else in the world. He had no doubt that Odysseus would kill him on a moment's notice, and since Odysseus was generally well-liked and he was not, he assumed Laertes was telling the truth.

Laertes was, in fact, telling a half-truth. In exchange for his service, Odysseus had extracted a promise from Agamemnon that Mycenean law and Mycenean forces would protect his wife and his lands while he was away. Unfortunately, Agamemnon was also away, and his wife, Clytemnestra, who had been left in charge, was too busy seducing her husband's arch enemy, Aegisthus, to worry about events on far away Ithaka.

The four men ate and drank in an awkward silence. Neither pair liked or trusted the other. Laertes glanced around the room and was relieved to see that Nexios had entered and was standing discretely in a corner where he could see everything that was going on.

After what seemed like an eternity, Penelope entered the room. All four men jumped to their feet. She was stunning in a diaphanous gown that sparkled with tiny gems and was set off by a ruby and lapis lazuli necklace that fell from her long white neck and came to rest between her ample, nearly completely exposed breasts.

All four men gasped and stood wordless in her presence.

"Polybus," Penelope said softly, "Is something amiss? Please speak. I have never known you to be so shy. Does my appearance displease you?"

"No, no," he stammered, "not at all. No, you are…" then finding the right word, he almost shouted it out, "Magnificent! You are magnificent! I have always admired your beauty and your grace, but today you are beyond words. I can see why Odysseus chose you over Helen."

"You flatter me, Polybus, but I am happy that you are pleased. I mean to please you today."

Polybus could barely contain himself. The promise contained in those words was more than he could have hoped for. When he received his invitation, he knew that he had Penelope cornered, that she would have to deal with him. He knew her financial position, and he had every intention of exploiting it to his advantage. He would take revenge upon his old enemy; he would take his land, and yes, even his wife, but he had never expected that she would come to him willingly. The idea that he could possess her wholly, that she would give herself to him—that was a dream that he never believed possible to achieve. But she had hinted that it was possible. "I mean to please you today," she had said. What a world of delight was contained in those words. Polybus was lifted to heights of bliss that he had never experienced before. He had visions of him and Penelope, like two young lovers, walking through the grounds, sitting in the garden, stepping into the bedroom. The fact that he was almost twice her age—that and all other impediments to his fantasy melted away with the words, "I mean to please you today."

The others were talking as Penelope led them into the dining hall, but Polybus didn't hear anything that was said. He was too deep into his dream world to pay attention to anything but his own fantasy.

When they sat down to eat, Polybus noticed Charis, Demia's companion had joined them and taken a seat between him and his son. This pleased him. It would give his son someone to talk to and keep him from interfering with his conversation with Penelope. Charis was older than Demia, but still attractive enough to hold Eurymachus' attention throughout dinner.

Eurymachus was a great disappointment to his father. Polybus had raised himself from nothing to great wealth. It appeared that his son was determined to lower himself back into poverty. He had neither brains nor ambition. He drank, gambled, and chased every woman he saw. He had taken up with the deceitful servant Melantho, who seemed intent on spending every penny Eurymachus had, or could get from his father. And recently, he had decided that he was in love with Illotos' wife Demia. It seemed to make no difference to him that she was in her ninth month of pregnancy, and might be, at this very moment, giving birth and possibly dying in the process.

Oh well, he thought, *maybe he'll fall in love with Charis and forget all about Demia.*

Polybus was lost in thought about his son, when he realized that Penelope had been talking to him, or at least, trying to.

"Do you find my appearance so displeasing, or my conversation so tedious, that you choose to ignore me?" She asked, feigning indignation, then softening it with a coy smile.

Polybus was embarrassed. He flushed a deep red and offered a copious and confusing array of apologies. Laertes observed the exchange and smiled. *Poor Polybus*, he thought. *He is in way over his head.*

Polybus was a no-nonsense, rough and ready street brawler who pulled himself up by trampling down everybody else. But he was totally out of place in Penelope's sophisticated world. He had no idea of how to act in such an environment. Penelope could play him like a lute, and once she realized the depth of his desire for her, she knew she could manipulate him at will.

"I am sorry if my words caused you embarrassment," she said. "You are my guest. It was rude of me to discomfort you. Please, relax. The meal will be presented shortly. We will eat, and then we may speak as friends."

No sooner had Penelope mentioned the word, 'dinner' than a bevy of servants appeared carrying trays of fruits, vegetables, and various forms of grains. However, the centerpiece of the table was a large swordfish, only recently pulled from the sea.

"I had Philoctius get up very early to go to town to buy the freshest, finest, fish available. I hope it is acceptable."

"It is more than acceptable, my Queen; it is outstanding."

Once aroused, Polybus' love of food permitted no time for anything else other than indulgence. He spoke no more through the entire meal which moved from fish to lamb to sweets to cheese, and then, finally, to sweetened wine, whose appearance signaled the end of the feast.

He pushed back in his chair, emitted a loud burp, and wiped his greasy hand and face on a wet cloth that had been handed to him by a servant. When she first presented it to him, he wasn't quite sure what to do with it, but he observed Penelope and Laertes using similar cloths to clean their hands, and he followed suit. Eurymachus, being far less observant than his father, simply wiped his hands and face on his garment.

When everyone was cleaned up and relaxed, Penelope opened the conversation.

"I understand that you have many contacts in Mycenae. Is that true?" she asked.

"I have business dealings throughout the Greek world," he answered, eager to prove his worth.

"Tell me," she said, "What news you hear from Troy. I am afraid that here, on this small island, we get very little news at all."

"The news from Troy is bad," he answered.

"Bad? How?"

"There has been talk of a major battle. They say many Greeks have died. There is even a rumor that Achilles is dead."

"A rumor?"

"Yes. It is just that, but it is widely credited."

"Who says this?"

"Traders and others."

"And do you believe this rumor?"

"It doesn't matter what I believe. The merchants and bankers believe it, and it has caused them to curtail credit."

"I do not understand."

"It is fear that motivates them. They have extended a great deal of money to King Agamemnon and the others on the belief that there would be a quick and easy victory. But now it seems that the victory, if it comes at all, will be neither quick nor easy, and so they grow fearful and recall their loans."

"And when their creditors can't pay?"

"They keep the collateral—which in your case, is your land. You see I know your situation, and I am eager to help. That is why I accepted your invitation."

"But the bankers are no farmers. What do they want with the land?"

"Nothing. They will sell it to the highest bidder."

"I am surprised that there would be any bidders. Who has the ready money available to buy these properties?"

"There are some."

"You?"

"Yes."

"And so, you will buy up properties cheaply while the owners are away at war."

"Yes."

"Some would think that unkind."

"Others would think it wise."

"It may surprise you, but I agree with the latter group. I am not a man, and so I have little understanding of these things, but it seems to me to be a wise thing to purchase property cheaply when you can."

"My Lady, you amaze me. I had thought to find you bitter that your husband left you at the mercy of bankers."

"Do not misjudge me or Odysseus. The world knows that he did not want to go to war and that he tried every way possible to avoid it without dishonor. But he owes allegiance to the King, and Agamemnon gave him no choice. I love my husband and will stay true to him for as long as he lives, but war is cruel, and Ares spares no one, not even kings. He may be lost already. If Achilles is truly dead, then there is little hope for any Greek. And if Odysseus is gone along with Achilles, then I must look after my son."

Polybus was delirious with joy. If this was not an invitation to a liaison, then he knew nothing of women.

"Madam," he said in the most sincere, effusive manner that his drunken state would allow, "I would be honored if you allow me to be of assistance in your time of need."

"That is very kind of you," she said as she dabbed a small tear away from the corner of her eye.

"Madam..." he began.

"Call me Penelope, please."

"Of course, Penelope..." He paused to reflect upon how grand it was to say her name aloud. How many times had he whispered it to himself in the dark of night? "...How can I help?"

"As I have said. I am a mere woman and know little of these things, But Philoctius knows what must be done, and Laertes has been my constant support. I trust these men completely. They will explain things that I do not understand. It is my fervent desire that you can reach some agreement with them that will allow us to continue to meet. I have enjoyed tonight's dinner and hope you can join us again."

"I would like nothing better—Penelope."

"I am tired and will take my leave so you gentlemen can talk. Good evening—Polybus."

* * *

As soon as she was able, Charis ran from Penelope's house to Demia's. She had just spent the worst night of her life being pawed at and drooled over by the most odious man she had ever met. She felt dirty. But she had done her job. She had kept Eurymachus from butting into Penelope's conversation with Polybus. She hoped it was worth the effort.

Dealing with Eurymachus was bad enough, but the entire time she was at the table, she thought about and worried over Demia. The poor girl had been in hard labor for almost two full days. Charis didn't want to leave her, but Eurycleia had convinced her that there was nothing she could do to help Demia, and she would be of more use at Penelope's. So she went, but she didn't stay a moment longer than was absolutely necessary.

Charis raced into the house and went directly to the bedroom where Demia lay. What she saw stopped her dead. Demia was lying motionless in the middle of a blood-soaked bed. Eurycleia was holding an armful of bloody rags.

"Is she...?"

"Sleeping," Eurycleia answered. "I gave her a potion. The poor thing was exhausted. She should sleep until noon."

"And the child?"

Eurycleia smiled a gap-toothed smile. "Children you mean—two of them, and from the look of them, we will need two wet nurses. They were bawling for milk from the moment they popped out."

"Twins!"

"A boy and a girl."

"Where are they?"

"In the next room, sleeping thank the gods."

"Can I see them?"

"Of course, but don't wake them. I am too tired to take care of them."

She sat down in a chair facing the bed, closed her eyes, and in less than a minute was sleeping as soundly as Demia. The two women, one young, one old, were both completely worn out. Charis wondered whether either would live to see the next day's sun. She walked to the bed and looked down at Demia. *She is so young*, she thought, and offered a prayer to Hera, the goddess of the home, to protect her. Then she left the two women and went in to see the children. Seeing her enter, a maid put her finger to her lips indicating that Charis should be quiet. *They are sleeping*, she mouthed.

Charis looked at the two babes, thought about Eurymachus, who peppered her with questions about Demia the whole time he was groping her, and shuddered.

* * * *

A Difficult Decision

It had been a week since the battle at the barricade, and Illotos still could not stand without help. His wounds had been severe and would have no doubt been fatal but for the action of Lipos, who threw himself over the fallen Illotos and kept him from being trampled by the Trojan cavalry. Most of the horses, seeing Lipos' large bulk in front of them and thinking it some sort of rock or obstacle, decided to jump over it or go around it. One reckless charioteer tried to go over Lipos, but only managed to overturn his chariot and die at the hands of Snake, who was also sheltering under Lipos' protective mass.

Odysseus found Illotos sitting upright on his cot berating a servant who was trying to change his bandages. The woman paid no attention to his grumblings and remained focused on her task.

"I see that you have recovered enough to complain about your treatment," Odysseus said.

"It is not the treatment," Illotos responded. "It is the boredom—and the fear that I will miss out on the next battle. I owe these Trojans something."

"Then I am afraid that I have some bad news for you."

Illotos reacted with alarm. "The surgeons have said that I will be fit to fight again," he blurted out. "My wounds will heal!"

"Yes, they will, but not in time."

"In time for what? What do you mean?"

"We are running out of food—and men. Their provinces supply them with both. Look around you. What do you see? It is the same in every Greek camp. We have lost too many men."

"The Trojans have lost men too!"

"They can replace them. We cannot. Nestor's spy reports that Aeneas has ordered his troops back from the eastern frontier. They will arrive within two weeks. That is all the time we have. It is just as well. Our food will barely last that long."

"What are you saying?"

"Once those troops arrive, Aeneas can bide his time. He can wait until we are so weak from hunger that we cannot lift our spears to defend ourselves. He can choose the time and the place of our slaughter."

"So, we must attack him before his forces arrive, while he is still weak."

"Illotos. Have I not always cautioned you to think before you speak?"

Illotos frowned. He was a man now, not a child. But he had to admit that Odysseus was right. There was no way the Greeks could launch an attack in their weakened state, and even if they could, the walls of Troy had proven their strength.

"What is left to us then? To sail home in disgrace? I would rather die here, with a sword in my hand."

"Spoken like a true Greek. I am proud of you Illotos. I want you to know that. You have proven your worth and rewarded my trust in you."

"But? There is more to this Odysseus. Out with it."

"The Council agrees with you. We will stay and die with honor, but..."

"But?"

"But they have also decided that those who are not fit to fight must be sent home..."

"NO!"

"Yes. Those who cannot fight consume food and require men to care for them. We can spare neither."

"Do not do this to me Odysseus. Do not shame me. Let me stand in line between Lipos and Snake and let me die with my comrades."

"If you could stand and hold your own, I would let you. But you cannot stand. Your friends would have to hold you up. And how are they supposed to defend themselves while they do that? You are being selfish Illotos. You are sending your friends to an ignoble death just so that you can die thinking yourself a hero."

"That is not so! I am not thinking of just myself; I am thinking of Demia. How is she to live with the shame? And what about my child? How will it grow up strong and proud if I am shamed?"

"How will either survive if your bones are left to bleach on the sand? Have you thought about your wife and child? Do you care if she lives or dies? Or do care only for your fame?"

"Not my fame! My reputation!"

"Think less of yourself Illotos and think more of your family. There are enemies at home as well as here, and in truth, you are needed there more than you are here. Here you will be just one dead body amongst many. There you may serve some useful purpose.

"You know that the gods offered Achilles the choice between a long life and a peaceful death surrounded by his children and grandchildren, and a short, glorious life with no offspring. And you know what he chose. I had thought that you had chosen the other path. Have your forgotten your Demia so soon? Do you not want to hold your child in your arms? Do you not see the glory in protecting them from the vipers who pray that you do not return? I tell you Illotos, I envy your opportunity. I wish that I were in your place. I would not hesitate to go home to Penelope and Telemachus. My heart aches to see them and to hold them close.

"You speak of glory. Have you not seen enough of war to know that it is not glorious? Look around you Illotos. What glory is there here?"

Illotos didn't need to look around to know that Odysseus was right. He was surrounded by the wounded and the dying. The smell of death permeated the entire room, and the sound of coughing, choking, dying men assaulted his ears from morning till night.

"I have not forgotten Demia. I think of her all the time. Sometimes I think that it is only the thought of her that keeps me alive in this hellhole they call Troy. I struggle to live in the hope that I will see her and my child before I die."

"Why, then, do you hesitate?"

"I fear the look of shame on her face when I step off the ship while you and the others remain here. I would rather die here and now then see that I have disappointed her."

"Do not worry about that, Illotos. The only look on her face will be joy when she sees you have returned alive. And you can forget about stepping off the ship. The surgeons tell me that you won't be walking for several weeks, and then only with a limp or a cane. I am afraid your days of winning laurel crowns are over. And as for shame—you have no fear of that. Your scars will answer to all that have the courage to challenge you."

"And if they do not suffice, my sword will answer for me."

"Well spoken. Are you content?"

"It is not the way I had hoped to return home, but it is for the best—and there is no alternative. Sometimes we must bend our will and accept what the gods have given us. I cannot say that I am content, but I will do as you direct. What is the plan?"

"A ship is being outfitted. It will carry the wounded, and I have assigned a dozen able-bodied men for its protection. It is not much, but it is the best I can do. I have selected older men with wives and families. And I am sending Lipos along to lead them."

"Lipos? Really?"

"Yes. I have promoted him to sergeant, and the men respect him."

"Will wonders never cease. When do we leave?"

"With the evening tide."

* * * *

The Trojan Horse

Odysseus watched the ship until it was lost beyond the darkness of the horizon. How he wished he were on it! He longed to see his wife and child, to walk in the quiet of his Ithakan home and sleep with his wife beside him in the large oaken bed he had made for her. That would be bliss. But that was not to be. Illotos was going home to life on Ithaka, and he was staying put, facing near-certain death in Troy.

'Near certain,' not 'absolutely certain,' not if Odysseus had anything to say about it. He turned from the sea and walked into Nestor's tent. He found the old man sitting quietly, sipping wine, so deep in thought that he hadn't noticed Odysseus enter. So he was startled when Odysseus spoke.

"I have a plan," he said.

"Of course you do," Nestor replied. "I have been waiting for you to come by. You've taken your time about it."

"Do you wish to hear it?"

"Certainly, but please sit and take a cup of wine." Odysseus sat, and Nestor poured a cup of wine, tipped it, and let a drop fall to the floor. "In honor of our ancestors," he said, "and those who will be left behind."

"Do we drink to ourselves, then? For it is likely that we will be among those left behind."

"If you believed that, you would not be here. Speak. I am eager to hear your plan."

"That spy of yours—What's his name?"

"Sinon."

"Yes, that's him. He is an artist, is he not?"

"Yes, and a very good one at that. Have you seen the horse he made for Patroclos?"

"No. I have not, but I have heard of it and was hoping that you could show it to me."

Nestor did not ask why Odysseus wanted to see the horse. He assumed that he would learn the reason when Odysseus felt it was necessary to tell him.

"Of course I can. After the deaths of Patroclos and Achilles, Agamemnon took the horse for himself because Calchas told him it was important. Nobody understands anything Calchas says, including Agamemnon, but if Calchas says it, Agamemnon does it."

"So it is in Agamemnon's tent?"

"Yes, but we can go and look at it. No one will stop us."

"Good! Let us do it then."

"Now?"

"Yes. Is there a problem?"

"We haven't finished our wine."

* * *

"I am no judge of art, but this is magnificent."

"Yes," Nestor agreed, "it is one of the most ingenious works of art that I have ever seen."

"The horse looks alive. It looks like it is ready to leap off its pedestal and carry a rider into battle."

The horse was created to scale, and finely carved in every detail. The wood was then scraped so that it resembled hair, and the whole thing highly polished. The mouth was slightly open, revealing two rows of perfect, slightly yellowed teeth. The nostrils were flared and ever so slightly tinged with red. The eyes were two red rubies, giving the horse an angry, frightening appearance, and was clad in the bronze armor of a war horse.

"Will it suit?" Nestor asked.

"Suit what?" Odysseus replied.

"Whatever purpose you have in mind for it. I am sure you didn't take me away from my wine to discuss art."

Odysseus began. "We cannot storm the gates, and we cannot sit and wait for Aeneas and his reserves to arrive to slaughter us. So we must do something..."

"Diomedes wants to lead an assault on the walls. I think he believes that if he huffs and puffs, he can blow the walls down."

"Diomedes is a fool."

"So are most men. a good many would follow him."

"Yes, I believe you are right. A good many *would* follow, especially since they all believe they are going to die anyway, and an arrow through the heart is not a bad way to go. But suppose we gave them an alternative—a chance, even a small one, that they might survive, and we may yet take this citadel and go home bathed in glory?"

"They would jump at it, as would I."

"This horse is a beauteous thing. I don't believe I've ever seen anything like it before."

"Odysseus, you are truly frustrating. What is your plan? And what does this horse have to do with it?"

"Suppose we could get a man inside this horse. Do you think your artist could hollow out a space for him?"

"It would have to be a very small man, but I'm sure that Sinon could do it."

"Good. And does the Great King have Hector's armor?"

"He does."

"Good. Here is my plan. We strike camp and sail away, leaving behind this horse and Hector's armor in tribute to the Trojans."

"I don't see how this helps us."

"Once beyond the headland we turn our ships to the delta of the River Scamander and make our way back under the cover of darkness to the walls outside the River Gate."

"I still do not understand."

"The Trojans will see that we have sailed off and left them a parting gift. They will accept Hector's armor—how could they not? You agree?'

"Yes."

"And they will also accept the gift of this beautiful horse."

"Probably, but I still don't see how that helps us."

"The horse will contain a man—and that single man will open the River Gate to our troops, and those troops will destroy Troy."

Nestor thought for a long time before he spoke. "This plan," he said, "is ingenious, but it has little chance of success. You have to hope that the Trojans accept the gift and bring it inside the wall. I wouldn't. I'd burn it where it stands."

"Yes, but you are wise. The Trojans will have seen us sail off. They will see that we have left Hector's armor behind. They will not think. They will take the bait."

"And what about the man that you intend to put inside the horse. He will have to be an extraordinary person, strong, disciplined, with absolute self-control."

"I have just the person."

"And then this person has to get out of the horse unseen, make his way from wherever he is to the River Gate, kill the guards and open the gate."

"Exactly."

"You believe this can be done?"

"No, but it's the only plan I have. Do you have a better one?"

"No. I will set Sinon to work immediately. Send your man to me tomorrow morning. I will show him the map of Troy. He will have to memorize it."

"He will be there tomorrow."

"There is one thing more."

"What is that?"

"Patroclos placed Sinon in charge of the Apollonian priestesses, Pythia and Phemenoe, and he is terrified of Agamemnon who has his men searching for the women."

"How does this affect me?"

"You need Sinon's cooperation. Offer him and the women your protection, and you will have it."

"Tell Sinon that from this moment he and the women are under my protection. I will send Kretin and a troop of soldiers to bring the women to my quarters.

* * *

Snake was not surprised to be summoned to Odysseus' tent. He was certain that he had done something wrong. If he hadn't, he reasoned, Odysseus would have included him, along with Lipos, to accompany Illotos home. After all, the three men had been friends for years and were virtually inseparable. The fact that he had been left behind did not bode well for him. He could not think of what he had done wrong, but, as he had spent his entire life more or less doing things wrong and causing trouble, he was resigned to the fact that he had, once again, screwed up.

So he was completely surprised when Odysseus asked him to sit down and a servant poured him a cup of wine.

He was completely confused. This was totally outside the range of his experience. He stared down at the cup of wine that had been placed before him, and it suddenly came to him—poison!

Whatever he had done must have been so heinous that Odysseus had brought him here in order to watch him drink hemlock. He had heard of such things—kings ordering their servants and underlings to kill themselves, but he never knew of it actually happening to anyone, and then to have it happen to *him*, and by *Odysseus*! He might have understood it had the order been given by Agamemnon, or Diomedes, the one was mad and the other cruel, but *Odysseus*?

He thought about it. He knew Odysseus to be fair, and just—and merciful. So he concluded that he deserved this punishment, and would accept it like a man.

Odysseus had been watching Snake's odd behavior. "Is there something amiss?" he asked.

"I will drain this cup to the lees, if you will but grant me one request," Snake responded, never once casting his eyes up to meet Odysseus'.

Odysseus was puzzled. He could not understand what was wrong with Snake, but he answered, "Speak. What do you want to know? If I can fulfill your request, I will."

"Then tell me what I have done to deserve this punishment?"

Odysseus was even more confused than he had been before. At first, he blurted out, "Punishment? What punishment?" but then he realized—"You think the cup is poisoned! And that I have summoned you here to your death!"

"It is not poisoned?"

"No."

"And I am not to die?"

"No."

Snake was so relieved that he took the bowl of wine between his trembling hands and drank it down in one continuous swallow, spilling half of it down his neck and arms as he did so.

"Do you feel better now?" Odysseus asked when he thought that Snake had regained his composure.

"Yes Sir!" he said, jumping to his feet and standing at attention. "I apologize, sir, for making such a fool of myself, sir!"

"At ease, soldier. The fault was mine, not yours. I should have explained to you the purpose of your visit here, which when you learn the truth of it, you might think the poisoned cup a better choice. I have a job for you."

"What is it Sir?"

"It is difficult to explain. It is best if I show you. Come with me."

Odysseus led Snake to a tent which served as an artist studio/workshop for Nestor's spy, Sinon. Nestor was there, watching as Sinon worked on the statue of a horse that he had created for Patroclos. Snake was stunned when he saw it.

"It looks real," he said in astonishment.

"How did you get Agamemnon to give it up?" Odysseus asked.

"That was easy," Nestor replied. "Sinon said that he had to add more jewels to the saddle. It will be harder to get him to give up Hector's armor. I have spoken to him about it, but he is adamant. It is the greatest trophy of the war. He intends to keep it."

"Tell him the Trojans will strip it from him after they kill him."

"I have told him, but he will not listen to reason."

"He listens to Calchas?"

"Yes."

"Then speak to Calchas. He is no fool, no matter what everyone thinks."

Snake was not used to speaking in front of people like Odysseus and Nestor, but he couldn't control his curiosity.

"Why am I here?" he asked. "Why show me this wondrous horse?"

Nestor and Sinon exchanged smiles. "This horse," Odysseus said, "will be your home for 24 hours. That is the job I told you about."

Snake screwed up his face. "I do not understand," he said.

"We have a plan," Odysseus explained, "which, if it works, will allow us to take the citadel and return home in glory."

"And this plan requires me to live in a wooden horse for 24 hours?"

"Yes. We will strike our tents and sail away, leaving behind this horse and Hector's armor…"

"The Trojans," Sinon continued, "will take these as gifts inside the walls…"

"We hope," added Nestor.

"They will." Sinon said. "Aeneas would rule against it, but Aeneas is not here. He has gone to the eastern provinces to raise the reinforcements. They will bring the horse inside the walls, and you with it."

"It will not be easy," Odysseus said. "You will be alone and cramped up inside this horse. If you make a sound, or are otherwise discovered, they will kill you on the spot."

Snake looked from one man to the other, wondering who was going to speak next.

It was Odysseus. "We will sail away in the afternoon after sacrificing to the gods. We want to make sure the Trojans see that we are making the proper preparations for departure. The horse and the armor will be left on the strand. Once out of sight, we will turn our ships around the headland and sail back into the mouth of the Scamander. From there we will march to the walls of Troy and wait for you to open the gate for us. Once the gate is open, your task is done. The rest is up to us."

"So, all I have to do is to crawl inside that horse, wait for dark, and open a gate? Sounds easy enough."

* * *

Snake waited until the last possible minute before climbing into his 'berth' inside the horse. Sinon had done his best to make the space as roomy and comfortable as possible, but there wasn't much he could do. He had placed some cushions around the interior, but they had to be very thin—space was at a premium. Snake was curled into a fetal position. He could not move his legs at all and could move his arms only a little. A dagger had been laid across his chest. It would be his only weapon, but it was one that Snake was especially adept at using. Because of his small size, he was at a disadvantage with the large, heavy swords and shield carried by Greek soldiers. However, there was no one better at in-close, hand-to-hand combat than Snake, who was quick and deadly with the shorter dagger, like the one that now rested on his chest. Two gourds had also been placed on his chest, one with water and the other containing a potion made from lotus leaves. He could bring these from his chest to his lips, but not easily. He had been told to sip the water, and not take too much at one time. The potion was to be taken only if the pain became unbearable. He did not understand this. The 'berth' was tight, but not much less comfortable than the trenches he had been sleeping in. He lay face up and breathed through a series of small holes drilled into the horse just under the bronze saddle. The air holes would only be visible if the entire bronze saddle were removed.

He heard voices, Greek voices, some giving directions, others grumbling. He felt himself being lifted up, then put down, and then moved. He assumed that the horse had been placed upon some sort of moving platform. Based on the grunts he was hearing, the horse was heavy. It wasn't long before it came to rest, and the Greek voices receded. He knew the sounds of sailing well enough to know, even at some distance, that ships were pushing off from shore, and striking their sails. He could hear the drums and knew that the oarsmen were at their stations, beating the waves in rhythm. He wished he were with them.

For a while there was only silence. He had an itch on his nose, but he couldn't reach it. He wanted to stretch out his legs, but he was unable to move them. *What was taking those damn Trojans so long? It must have been an hour since the Greeks sailed away.* It was getting hot inside the horse, even though the sun had set and a cool breeze was blowing off the sea. Snake was sweating and uncomfortable, but his 'berth' allowed him no room for movement. He lifted his head as close to the air holes as he could and gluttonously sucked in the fresh sea air.

He heard voices, at first only two, then several, coming closer. He imagined their amazement. He visualized them walking around the magnificent horse, praising its beauty. Oddly, they kept their distance. Then he realized why—they were afraid of it! He heard the word 'trick,' along with several derogatory, gross comments about 'Greeks.' He grew angry and wished

that he could leap out and cut the tongues out of the
Trojans, but Odysseus had made it clear: His mission
was to remain hidden until he could emerge unseen and
open the gate.

The murmurings continued for what seemed an
eternity. The itch on his nose tormented him. His limbs
ached, he thought that if he could not stretch out, he
would go mad. He felt like he had been confined for
days. *What are these trojans doing?* He wondered. He got
his answer: They were waiting for people of authority to
decide what to do. There was a clatter of chariots and a
chorus of shouts. Someone in armor approached and
walked around the horse, rapping his knuckles on the
wood to test its density. Snake, who could hear the
clinking of the bronze as the man circled the horse,
pulled himself tighter into a ball and held his breath.

Sinon had anticipated this and left the horse as solid
as he could. He could have allowed Snake more room,
but if he had, then the hollow sound would be apparent
to anyone like the man circling the horse now. His
precautions paid off. the man declared the horse safe,
and immediately four men stepped forward, lifted it off
its pedestal, and began carrying it to the city.

In addition to being hot, in pain, and tortured with
assorted pinches and itches which he could do nothing
about, Snake was starting to get seasick from the uneven
rocking motion as the four men carried the horse up the
beach across a gradually rising grassy slope and finally
through the gate into the city where it was greeted by a

joyous, raucous mob already half-way to delirium, celebrating their victory over the hated Greeks.

Snake was feeling nauseous. His stomach rumbled, and he farted loudly. Fortunately, the mob was making so much noise that nobody heard him, and he was left alone in his 'berth' with only his pain, the heat, and now the foul odor of his own excretions. He pushed his face closer to the air holes and prayed for death.

The city had gone wild. He couldn't see it, but he could hear it. There was music and singing, at least he thought that's what it was—there was really too much noise to be sure about any of it. Mostly it was just yelling and shouting. He hated it. It had been several hours now that he had been in what he was rapidly beginning to think was his coffin, and he didn't know how much longer he could stand it. It seemed to him that he had been entombed for days. The pain in his joints was becoming unbearable, as was the heat. He sipped at his water gourd, but it did little to relieve his thirst and nothing for his pain. The blanket that Sinon had installed for his comfort clung to his skin and itched. He had to urinate.

The noise continued unabated. He became dizzy. He thought if he didn't stretch out, he would scream. He cursed the heat, the Trojans, Odysseus, and anything else he could think of. Then he remembered his other gourd, the one Odysseus told him contained the Lotus leaf potion. Odysseus had told him to take some if the pain became too great. *STUPID! Why hadn't he thought of it sooner?* He wiggled his fingers into position to grab hold of it, but it had slipped down off his chest onto his side, and he couldn't reach it.

He squirmed and wriggled until he could get his fingers around the string that held the gourd closed. Bolts of pain shot up his arm as he maneuvered the gourd into place. Sweat poured down from his head into his eyes. Every inch of his body itched and ached. He frantically tried to bring the gourd to his lips, but he couldn't quite make it. He squeezed the gourd in desperation, and a stream of liquid spurted out striking him in the face and running down his cheeks. Tears streamed from his eyes. He tried again, this time issuing a scream as he sprung his arm free and raised the gourd to his lips. Odysseus had told him to take only a small drink of the potion, but he was nearly delirious. He took one drink and then another. He felt almost immediate relief. His pain diminished and eventually evaporated completely. He became drowsy, and soon fell fast asleep.

* * *

When he woke, he had no idea where he was. He instinctively tried to move but found that he could not. His mind was fuzzy. He couldn't think straight. He knew who he was, and he knew that he was supposed to be doing something. He even remembered that Odysseus had asked him to do it, but he couldn't remember what it was, and what was even more annoying, he couldn't figure out what he was doing rolled into a fetal position in a confined area. He knew very little for certain, but he was absolutely sure of one thing—he had to piss, and badly.

The pain in his kidneys was growing by the minute. He was going to have to urinate soon. He couldn't hold it much longer. He saw a lever just over his head, and realized, without knowing how or why, that he should pull on it. He did, and the floor beneath him tipped silently downward. He slid down headfirst, exiting the horse headfirst, like a newborn baby. He rolled gently onto the ground and released an agonizing burst of urine. It arched in a steady stream from his loins directly onto the chest of a man who stood wide-eyed, having just watched a wooden horse giving birth to a human—or, as he supposed, a god in human form.

The man made no effort to say or do anything. He absorbed his urine bath without comment, staggered backward a few steps, turned, and walked away on unsteady limbs.

Snake watched him wobble away. He looked around. He was laying on the ground underneath what appeared to be a statue of a horse in the middle of a vast plaza. He heard a sound, which, at first, he did not recognize, but when he heard it repeated, he knew it to be snoring—someone was sleeping close by.

He tried to move, but the slightest attempt sent shooting pains through his joints. He managed to tip his head enough to see that the snoring was coming from a soldier who was propped up against the legs of the statue, sound asleep. None of this made any sense to Snake. He studied the soldier. And then it all came back to him. *A Trojan! The soldier was a Trojan! And he had been stuffed inside the horse by Odysseus so he could get inside the city and open the gates. And it had worked! He was inside the city, but what next?*

Snake lay there, curled up, studying his surroundings—as much of it as he could see from his cramped position. He strained to remember what Nestor had shown him of the city. Given the size of the plaza that was open to his sight, he concluded that he must be in the center of town at what the Trojans called their 'Forae,' or meeting place. He had cursed Nestor for making him recite everything over and over again, but now he knew the wisdom of it. He knew where he was, and he knew where he had to go. All he had to do now was to get his limbs to work.

He worked on his upper limbs first, starting with his hands, then moving to his forearms, until he was able to fully extend his arms. His elbows and shoulders hurt, but the pain seemed to lessen with each movement. Soon he was able to raise his arms high enough to close his escape hatch. He was less successful with his lower limbs, which seemed to have solidified in place during his confinement. He had no exact idea of the time, or how long he had been inside the horse, but he knew that he had entered it shortly before sunset, and now, judging by the constellations visible to him in the night sky, it was well past midnight—that meant six-to-eight hours locked in that uncomfortable embrace. No wonder his muscles and joints rebelled when he tried to move them.

He also knew that he had to get out of the middle of the plaza before the guard woke up. So he rolled over on his stomach and began to crawl away using his elbows and letting his useless legs drag along behind. It was a slow, arduous task, but it bore fruit. He began to feel tingling in his legs. Apparently, the work was making his blood circulate. He reached the edge of the plaza and propped himself up against the corner of a building.

This gave him a much better view of his surroundings. The "Forae' or plaza, was huge, much larger than anything he had seen, even in Mycenae. He also noticed that the place was littered with garbage and a few humans, either sleeping or dead, he could not tell which. *Must have been some party*, he mumbled to himself. He also noticed a number of others sleeping in doorways, or, like him, propped up against the side of a building. "*Good*, he thought, *if anyone sees me, they will think I am just another drunk.* The thought relaxed him. he felt out of danger and took the time to gently stretch his limbs. Two soldiers walked by, but they paid him no mind. He saw another soldier walk across the plaza to the statue, wake the sleeping guard, and take his place on duty. He thanked the gods that he been able to move before the second guard arrived.

Once he felt strong enough, he pulled himself up with the help of the stone wall and tested his legs. They were wobbly, but they worked. He began a stumbling, unsteady walk around the plaza, confident that if anyone saw him, they would think him just another drunk working his way home.

Nevertheless, he hugged the walls of the buildings, staying in their protective shadows as he circumnavigated the square. *No sense drawing attention to myself*, he thought. He knew where he was headed; he remembered Nestor's map. When he came to a large temple on one corner of the square, he turned to his right and followed a narrow lane that wound its way through a residential section of the city. He knew he was going in the right direction because the housing deteriorated as he ventured further and further from the main square—just as Nestor had predicted. The street he was following ended at the city wall. He peered around the corner. The street was empty with the exception of two guards who lounged lazily against the supporting columns of the River Gate. He had made it! Now, all he had to do was to figure out how to eliminate the guards.

He flipped the dagger from his chest to his back so the guards would not see it as he approached. Then he took a flask in each hand and staggered forward, swinging the flasks wildly. The guards looked at him as he approached and rolled their eyes.

The one closest to Snake took a step or two in his direction, his arms extended in friendship. "All right, old man," he said, but he got no further. Snake whipped the dagger from his back and shoved it up under his ribs until it hit his heart. He died without a sound, but his armor clinked as he sunk to the ground, and his companion, startled, tightened his grip on his spear and began to raise his shield in defense. But Snake had withdrawn the dagger before the first guard had even begun to fall and sent it flying through the air at the second guard. It struck him in the chest near his shoulder. The guard dropped his spear and grabbed at the dagger with both hands. Snake ran to him, placed both hands on his neck and squeezed until he was exhausted, and he was sure the man was dead. Then he took the man's sword and with a single blow cut the rope that held the counterweight. The rock fell; the gate rose, and Odysseus stepped through.

* * * *

The Fall of Troy

Odysseus paused long enough to make sure that Snake was attended to, then he and Kretin moved quickly, hoping to get to the palace in time to offer his protection to Cassandra. He had no doubt that she would need it. The Greeks had spent months on the beach, enduring wind, rain, and unbearable heat. They worked like slaves on the barricade, fought in two major battles, and done all this on starvation rations, without rest, and more importantly, without women. They were angry. They wanted revenge for their dead comrades, they wanted the booty they had been promised, most of all, they wanted women. There would be no mercy. The rules of war were simple. The males were killed; the women raped. Odysseus expected no less. Cassandra would need him.

Diomedes raged like a mad bull through the city, killing every man, woman, and child who crossed his path. He had no interest in rape. He only wanted blood. He headed straight for the palace, and once there, directly to the throne room where he found what he was looking for. Priam sat on his throne, flanked by his wife, Hecuba, and Hector's wife, Andromeda who clutched her infant son,

Astyanax, to her chest. The women were petrified with fear at the appearance of the bloody Greek warrior standing before them, but Priam sat emotionless, completely unaware of the danger he was in.

Diomedes roared and smacked his sword on his shield, sending a loud, metallic *clang* echoing around the room and down the halls of the palace, but Priam remained unmoved. It was not until Diomedes stood directly over him with his sword raised above his head that Priam's eyes opened wide in disbelief and fear, too late to avoid the blade's deadly descent. Diomedes cleaved Priam nearly in two, spraying blood and brains over the two women who sat beside him crying and screaming.

Diomedes took a deep breath and looked around the room for someone else to kill. Andromeda was weeping uncontrollably, squeezing little Astyanax to her breast. The infant let out a small whimper. Diomedes heard it, and his eyes fell on the child.

"*NO! NO!*" Andromeda screamed, but her cries only served to further enflame Diomedes' blood lust. He wrenched the child out of his mother's hands, tossed him in the air, and caught him on the end of his sword as he descended. He dropped the child's dead body in his mother's lap and left.

* * *

The palace was huge, and Nestor's map only laid out the way to the public rooms. The private quarters contained hundreds of rooms for the use of the royal family, guests, and servants. Odysseus and Menelaus searched these rooms, Odysseus for Cassandra and Menelaus for Helen.

Menelaus found Helen in a garden, sitting with Paris alongside a small pool fed by a fountain, and filled with small, multi-colored fish. Paris was dressed for battle and stood when Menelaus entered.

"You are barely more than a boy, an archer, not a soldier," Menelaus said. "Your skills are with the bow, not the sword."

"Barely more than a boy is still a man," Paris answered.

"I bear you no ill will," Menelaus said, "neither you nor Helen."

"Nor I you," Paris answered.

Helen jumped up from where she had been sitting. "Must this be?" she asked.

"You know it must, my love," Paris answered. "I will not be carried in a cage through the streets of Sparta to be laughed at and disgraced."

Helen dropped back down, hung her head and cried. She did not watch as Paris and Menelaus laid into each other. The battle was one-sided and brief.

When it was over, Menelaus approached Helen. "I want you to know," he said, "That I took no pleasure in his death. He died honorably. I hope that is some comfort."

"Kill me," Helen whispered. "Send me to Hades with my love."

"That cannot be," Menelaus responded.

"What then?" Helen managed to ask through her tears.

"You will return to Sparta as my queen and my wife, with all the respect and honor that attaches to those titles."

"How can this be after I have abandoned you?"

"You were taken against your will..."

"But..."

"Do not argue. If these men thought that you came here of your own free will, they would tear the both of us to pieces. They must never learn that all the suffering and death were for no purpose."

* * *

Odysseus wandered the halls of the palace, frantically searching for Cassandra. The palace guards had all been slaughtered by Diomedes, and the servants had fled, so there was no one to ask. They went from room to room in the huge complex but could find no trace of Cassandra.

Almost in despair, they turned into a narrow corridor that led away from the main part of the palace and opened into what was clearly a guard's station. Odysseus recognized it immediately as a prison area within the palace complex, and when he heard women screaming, he knew he had found the right place.

He and Kretin followed the screams until they came to a large, oaken door. They barged through the door onto a scene of bloody horror. A group of six or seven men surrounded three women. Two were on the floor, having been raped and butchered. A third, Cassandra, lay on the bed in a pool of blood. Ajax Minor, who had just violated her, stood back from the bed and turned at the sound of Odysseus' entrance.

Odysseus took in the sight with horror and disgust. He let out a roar and threw his spear with such might that it went clear through Ajax Minor's chest and exited his back. The other men drew their swords, but Odysseus and Kretin made short work of them.

Odysseus went to Cassandra's side. Ajax Minor had raped her and then cut her belly open so that, even if she lived, she would not bear children.

Odysseus sat on the bed next to her and lifted her head, while Kretin went to work staunching the flow of blood from her wound.

"I am sorry, Princess," he said. "I am too late."

"Do not blame yourself," she whispered, "or even the filthy man who has done this to me. This was predicted. You could not have prevented it. It is the gods who are to blame. This is their doing."

"I will send for a surgeon. There may yet be time. You can return with me to Ithaka and live in peace."

"No, please. Let me die here in Troy along with my brothers. I do not wish to live any longer, and I fear that if I die in some foreign land, they will not be able to find me among the shades in the underworld."

"As you wish, Princess, but I could have wished for better."

"And I Odysseus. I had a moment," she said, "when I heard the men approaching...I thought it might be you and my heart leapt up, but it was just one more bitter trick..."

She was interrupted by a spate of coughing. Blood trickled from her lips. Odysseus glanced at Kretin, but he merely shook his head, 'no.'

She fell back and died, cradled in Oydsseus' embrace.

After a short while, Odysseus rose and turned to Kretin.

"We are done here," he said. "Gather the men. Provision the ships. We sail for home on the morning tide."

* * * *

THE END

OTHER BOOKS BY NEIL MARESCA

Angel is set in Jersey City in the 1950s, and introduces a kind-hearted tough guy named Ox Moran, his sidekick, the dwarf Stumpy, and a string of bad guys and beautiful women. *Angel* is the first in a series of Barbary Coast novels.

The Stolen Princess is the second book in the Barbary Coast series: Ox and Stumpy become embroiled in a Gracchi mob family feud while trying to help the dying *Capo*, Uncle Frank, rescue his kidnapped 16-year-old daughter.

Angie, the third book in the Barbary Coast series brings the Gracchi family saga to an end. Ox and the new capo, Angie, must deal with the homicidal Tommy the Hammer and a host of other mafia types before settling affairs in a shootout in an abandoned Jersey City railroad yard.

Appointment in Berlin takes readers back to the cold war era of the mid-1950's. It is the first in the series of Lucas Hamilton spy thrillers. It covers his early years as a child in war-torn Budapest, his harrowing escape from the Nazis and the Bolsheviks, and his introduction to undercover work.

Freedom's Dawn is the second in the series of Lucas
Hamilton spy thrillers. This book takes Lucas to South
Africa in 1957, where he must fight double-agents,
soviet operatives, and both native Africans and
Afrikaan extremists to prevent the country from falling
into chaos.

Mourning in Budapest, the third novel in the Lucas
Hamilton series, takes Lucas undercover in Hungary,
where he must deal with memories of his father's
assassination, and his childhood escape, along with new
threats from agents, double-agents, spies, informers,
and the dangerous, dark haired, dark-eyed Zsofia, who
puts a gun to his head and a hold on his heart.

Aphrodite's War is the first book in the Trojan War
cycle. When Paris, the Prince of Troy, falls madly in love
with Helen, the beautiful Queen of Sparta, he sets into
motion a cycle of greed, jealousy, and lust for power that
destroys the budding peace between the Trojan Empire
and the emerging Greek states, and sets the stage for the
events the whole world knows as the Trojan War, a
tragedy that draws into its web not only Helen and Paris,
but also the young lovers Illotos and Demia, Paris'
sister, the Princess Cassandra, and the hero, Odysseus,
who pines for peace and a quiet life with his wife and
new-born son.

The Fiery Sword, Well, Book I is the first of a two-part fantasy novel that follows the growth of 16-year-old Cassandra Allswell as she pits her courage and goodness against the evil power of the Malvolkian Queen Morgana in a fight for civilization's survival.

An Italian Journey is a light, humorous, and uplifting story about Nick and Laura Lobono and their fellow tourists that draws upon the author's personal experience and love of all things Italian.

Prospero is a modern adaptation of William Shakespeare's, *The Tempest*. Set in rural Montana in the 1960's, the book presents Shakespeare's Prospero, Miranda, Caliban, *et al.* in a new and different light.

Read excerpts from all Neil Maresca's books and gain free access to short stories and other material at: www.neilmaresca.com.

*** * * ***